The Secret
of the Stolen Mandolin

Answering a mysterious call for help, Phyllis, Hilary and their cousin Yop find the peace and quiet of their holiday shattered as they are whisked off on a journey to another world in search of a valuable stolen mandolin. As they set out to track down the elusive thief and solve the mystery of the forbidden island, they begin to realise that they have come to this new world for a special purpose of their own. It soon becomes clear that this is no ordinary adventure but a strange voyage of discovery.

The Secret
of the Stolen
Mandolin

Barbara Larkin

THE SECRET OF THE STOLEN MANDOLIN

Oneworld Publications Ltd
1c Standbrook House, Old Bond St, London W1X 3TD
P.O. Box 1908, Limassol, Cyprus

British Library Cataloguing in Publication Data
Larkin, Barbara
The Secret of the Stolen Mandolin
I. Title
813′.54(J) PZ7

ISBN 1–85168–003–9

Phototypeset by Input Typesetting Ltd, London
Printed in Great Britain by
The Guernsey Press Co. Ltd., Guernsey, C.I.

Contents

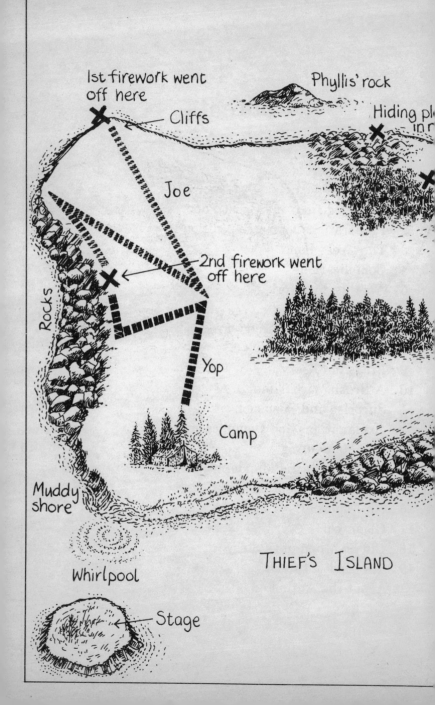

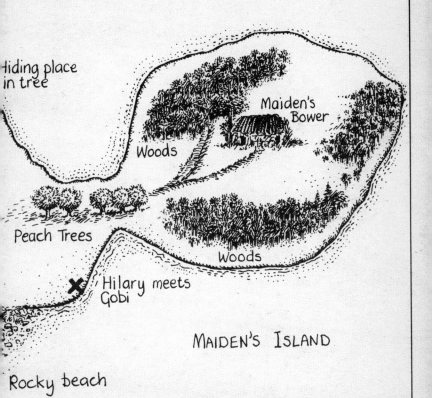

Hiding place
in tree

Woods

Maiden's
Bower

Peach Trees

Woods

✕ Hilary meets
Gobi

MAIDEN'S ISLAND

Rocky beach

1
The Frog from the Great Pond

'There's a frog in the filter!' cried Hilary. 'Grab him, quick!'

Her cousin Yop reached a freckled, sunburnt arm into the filter and fished around. 'Got him! No, he's too slippery . . . Get out of the light . . . I can't see him . . . uh!' And then suddenly the frog flew from his grasp and landed on the tiles at the edge of the pool.

'Oh, good, he should be safe now!' Hilary's little sister Phyllis ran forward, and the frog, in the idiocy of panic, leapt into the water. It was all Phyllis could do to resist the urge to jump in and swim after him.

'I'll get the net,' said Yop, and within a few minutes the poor weary amphibian was on the lawn. By this time Joe Harris, the gardener, had arrived.

'Maybe he's dead,' said Phyllis.

'I don't think so,' answered Yop. 'He was quite lively there in the pool a minute ago.'

'But he's not moving at all.'

'Maybe the chlorine has hurt him.'

'Or maybe he's just frightened.'

Joe Harris crouched down and looked carefully at the frog. 'Why don't we just leave him alone for now,' he suggested. 'You could come back later to see how he is.'

'Not that it really matters,' offered Hilary, 'because we can't do anything for him.'

And that was that. Or it would have been, except that Hilary couldn't forget about the frog, or believe, even though she had said it herself, that there was nothing to be done.

The girls' mother (who was Yop's Auntie Jane) brought out a snack of fruit and biscuits and cheese, and invited Joe to take a break and join them. Then Hilary went indoors and played video games, while Yop and Phyllis caught a few more butterflies for Yop's collection. Hilary checked the frog, but he was as still and silent as before.

The afternoon wore on. They swam for a while. Phyllis and Hilary both went to look at the frog again – no change.

Nobody cares about him, Hilary thought sadly. Somehow the fact that nobody cared (nor would solve anything by caring) made the frog's plight seem even worse. She went over to a group of pine trees and sat down in their shade. Behind her, from the side of the pool, she could hear the muffled sounds of listless late-afternoon conversation between Phyllis and Yop. The gardener, his work over for the day, was playing softly on a chubby guitar which he always carried with him. Everything seemed so ordinary and so peaceful that Hilary wished she could forget about the frog.

Why am I so silly? she thought. It's useless to worry about a stupid frog. There's nothing I can do for him, so I should put him out of my mind. Anyway, what does it matter whether he lives or dies?

The music behind her stopped, and she turned to see

Joe and Phyllis coming across the lawn toward her. Yop was stirring little circles in the water, probably watching the reactions of some poor beetle, or doing a scientific experiment on ripple effects.

'How's your frog doing?' called Joe, as he approached her.

Hilary shook herself mentally and physically, and stood up. 'I'll have one last look. Maybe we could move him down into the woods. Then, if he's alive, he won't have so far to go to the pond.'

'Good luck,' said Joe, as if he meant it, and went off around the house.

The frog was bigger.

They'll never believe me, thought Hilary, and looked harder.

'Phyllis! Come and look!' She turned and bumped into her sister.

'Is he dead?' asked Phyllis sadly.

'No, he's grown!' Hilary answered, and ran to get Yop. 'Come and see the frog!'

'Why should I?'

In the end, Hilary practically had to drag Yop across the lawn. 'You must come and see him,' she insisted, pulling at his arm.

Finally, hurrying rather reluctantly, Yop came over. 'So what?' he said, glancing absently at the frog. He waited patiently, his mind elsewhere. The various insects he had been playing with had all been dead, and he had been experimenting to see if dead insects float on their backs, like fish.

'Don't you notice anything different about him?' asked Hilary. She was shivering with impatience.

3

'Yeah, you're right! He's got purple spots! Wow!' said Yop sarcastically, and began to turn away.

'No, stupid, really! Look at him properly. He's bigger! Before he was sort of tucked down in the grass, and now he's practically on top of it.'

'Maybe it's just another frog,' suggested Phyllis.

'No, he's not,' snapped Hilary. 'I've been keeping an eye on him all afternoon – you saw him too, just a while ago – and he hasn't moved.'

The frog, who had been listening in frustration (he was a little short-tempered, what with spending an eternity in the filter, breathing chlorine), chose this moment to show a few purple spots, to speed things up a little.

Phyllis gasped. 'You're right, Yop, he *has* got purple spots! But I never saw them before!'

The frog blew out his bubble, goggled his eyes, grew a couple of inches, and flashed more spots.

What do you do under such circumstances? Do you stand there like a comedian, with your mouth hanging open? Do you burst with delight at the impossible? Or freeze in terror, wishing you could run?

What have I let myself in for now? thought Hilary wildly, backing up a little. 'This is weird,' she said. 'Don't touch him. Maybe he's got some disease.'

'Frog pox,' said Yop. 'Or maybe he's really a prince, and that's the royal purple showing through.'

The frog cleared his throat. They didn't learn until later that this was what he was doing. It sounded more like the rumble of thunder. A frog has a substantial throat to be cleared.

'I am not a prince,' he said. 'And I'm not sick, except from your horrid pool water! I have come from the Great Pond to seek your aid and assistance.' He spoke

4

very quickly in a strange, gurgly voice, and no one quite understood.

'I-I beg your pardon?' gulped Hilary.

'Listen, please listen,' said the frog.

'We *are* listening,' said Phyllis. She knelt before him. 'But you talk too fast for us.'

The frog repeated himself more slowly. 'Please come to the Pond,' he added.

'To the pond down in the woods?' asked Yop.

'Yes! Please say you'll come!' The frog turned as if to lead them down the path.

'But why?' continued Yop. 'What do you want us for?'

'We've never seen a talking frog before, you see,' said Phyllis. 'We need a little time to get used to you, and some sort of explanation as to what you want.'

The frog sighed, trying to control his impatience. 'The Maidenfrog's mandolin has been stolen. We need it desperately, or the Froggy Choir can't sing properly. It was stolen by a human, and we need your help to get it back. Come with me to the Great Pond. It will take none of your time. Just the blink of an eye, and you'll be back here again.' He goggled at them expectantly, as if all was now perfectly clear.

'We can't just get up and go,' said Hilary indignantly. 'What will our mother say?'

The frog's eyes bulged with agitation. 'No, no, she need never know! You'll be back here the instant after you leave.'

'Of course,' said Yop. 'It's like that in lots of books. Well, I never thought I'd get a chance to try it out!'

'That's the spirit!' said the frog. 'Will you come, then?'

'Maybe,' answered Yop. 'But first I want to know

5

more. What makes you think we can find this mandolin for you?'

'The human is stranded with the mandolin on an island in the Great Pond. We have his boat; he can't escape without our knowing, and he'll never be able to swim away with the mandolin. But when we try to approach him he shoots rockets at us. He might hurt a frog who tried to reason with him, but perhaps he'll listen to other humans! Let's go!'

The frog turned in the direction of the small pond at the bottom of the woods and, hesitantly, they all began to follow him.

'It takes no time at all,' chirruped the little creature as he hopped along. 'We just hold hands, down we go, and we're into the Great Pond.'

Hilary gasped, 'You don't mean you want us to go into that disgusting little pond down there, do you?'

The frog paused. 'Why, yes,' he said, 'but it's not such a bad little pond, and when you go through it you'll come to the paradise of music, the Great Pond!'

'Hilary! Phyllis! Yop! Suppertime!'

Hilary breathed a sigh of relief. She needed time to think. 'Let's go and eat, and talk this over properly.'

'But he needs help now!' cried Phyllis.

'And you need food,' insisted Hilary. 'I'm sorry, Phyllis, but you're not going with him until you've eaten.'

'But –'

'It's all right,' said the frog. 'I understand. You have to eat. I've waited all afternoon – I had no choice, as your pool made me so ill – and I can wait a little longer, as long as you promise me you'll come back. I'm impatient only because I must be certain you'll help me!'

Phyllis bent down to the frog. 'Wait for us at the pond,' she reassured him. 'I'm definitely coming back, and maybe they will, too. Don't worry.' She picked him up gently, and with only a twinge of repulsion, kissed him on the top of his head.

'I trust you,' he answered, blinking slightly at her caress. 'Dear child, we need you – really we do.'

'Now we *know* he's not a prince in disguise,' laughed Yop, as Phyllis set the frog back on the path. 'Don't worry, froggy, we'll see you soon.'

The three of them clambered up through the woods in a great hurry. They didn't usually respond so quickly to the call for supper.

'We can't just – just jump into this without thinking,' said Hilary after a minute.

Phyllis looked stonily back at her, and Yop smiled annoyingly.

'I'm sorry,' continued Hilary heatedly, 'but this isn't a book, it's real life, and one of us has to be responsible. Even if we arrive safely at this "Great Pond" – and there's no guarantee of that – who knows what will happen there? The thief can't be a very nice person! And how do we know if we'll ever get back again? There are other things to consider, too. Think of that little pond, for example. It's so full of muck and germs that we'll probably end up with all sorts of infections!'

'I don't care about infections!' retorted Phyllis. 'That frog needs us. I thought you cared about the frog. You've been watching him all afternoon.'

'I do care about the frog, but I care even more about you and Yop, and Mum, too. What would she say to all this? She'd never let you go!'

'If you dare tell her, I'll never forgive you – you traitor!' cried Phyllis.

7

'I can just imagine the scene,' chuckled Yop, 'if you tell Auntie Jane we saw a talking frog! Anyway, how could we miss such a terrific opportunity? This is definitely a once-in-a-lifetime chance.'

'Oh, Yop, you're right! I always imagined something like this happening, but now that it has, I don't know what to do!'

'Well, *I* know what to do!' Phyllis stormed on up the path.

'For the moment, let's try to behave normally,' said Yop. On that note they composed themselves and, surrounded by an aura of suppressed excitement, went into the house to eat.

2

Preparations for an Expedition

'I'm finished!' announced Phyllis. She laid down her knife and fork and wiped her mouth. 'May I go, please?'

'No, you may not,' said her mother. 'I've told you three times not to eat so fast. You can at least sit for a while to help your poor overworked stomach.'

Yop grinned and inwardly gave thanks for the time to finish his supper. As for Hilary, she seemed to need all the time she could get. She was so preoccupied that she had eaten only half of her usual healthy portion. For much of the meal she sat fingering her long brown hair, braiding and unbraiding it. Suddenly she seemed to make a decision, looked up, and asked, 'Can we go swimming again after supper, Mum?'

'Yes, of course, but just eat a little more, dear.'

Phyllis frowned and threw an angry glance at Hilary and then at Yop, as if to say, 'Are you going to back out, too?' Yop stared at her quite blankly, hoping that Auntie Jane wouldn't notice how excited and strung-up they all were. He wanted no hitches in the adventure to come. When his meal was finished, he laid down his knife and fork, folded his arms, and patiently waited for Hilary.

Soon they were on their way upstairs. Yop steered the resisting Phyllis (who wanted to go straight outside) into the girls' bedroom after Hilary, and shut the door.

'We can't go into that yucky pond without at least changing into our bathing suits,' said Hilary grumpily.

'You don't have to come if you don't want to,' retorted Phyllis.

'Yes, I do,' said Hilary. 'I can't tell Mum – she'd think I'm crazy – and I can't let you go alone, so what choice do I have? Don't say Yop will take care of you. He thinks all this is just a big game. Besides, I'm your sister, and I'm responsible for you.'

Yop laughed. 'Admit it, Hilary – you're coming because you don't want to miss all the fun!'

Hilary looked uneasy. 'Of course I don't want to miss a chance like this, but that doesn't make it right! And it doesn't make me any less scared.'

'I don't need a babysitter,' said Phyllis firmly but unconvincingly, hoping in her heart that Hilary would come along. 'I'm almost eight, and that's old enough to take care of myself.'

'Don't be silly,' said Hilary. 'Oh, I know you're brave, and everyone's always saying you're as sensible as someone twice your age, but I still have to come with you.' She straightened up and added decisively, 'We'd better make some preparations.'

'But we're just going into the pond and out again,' said Phyllis. 'You heard what the frog said.'

But Hilary was not so sure, and neither was Yop. 'If this Great Pond really exists,' said Yop, 'and if a frog can talk, anything is possible, then we have to think about the time we'll be spending *there*, not the time we *won't* be spending here. Where will we stay?

What will we eat?' His eyes shone with excitement. 'Just imagine! Different worlds, different dimensions of time . . .'

'Come back to earth,' said Hilary. Although we may not be here for long, she thought. 'We have to pack for camping. Then we'll be sure to have shelter. I don't suppose we could stay in a frog's house! Just the essentials – extra clothes, pup tent, jackknives, some food. Matches and candles in waterproof containers. But we can't possibly take sleeping bags.'

'How about my space blanket?' suggested Yop. He had ordered it through the mail. It was large but thin and light, and was supposed to keep you incredibly warm. 'It's lucky I didn't leave it at home. How could I have known I would need it during the summer holidays?'

'Come on then, let's hurry,' urged Phyllis.

Within a short time they had collected all the appropriate gear. Fortunately, the blanket was still in its sealed plastic cover. They put the matches, candles and clothes in plastic bags closed with twist ties, and for further safety put the matches in a plastic container.

'What about food?' asked Hilary.

'Why not some of Mum's health food bars?' said Phyllis. 'We won't have to sneak those out. Mum will be thrilled if we want some.'

Six yoghurt and nut bars were crammed into Hilary's knapsack with the other supplies. Yop carried the tent, with a strap to tie it around his waist. Inside the strap he slipped a hatchet.

'You can carry all the sandals, Phyllis,' said Hilary. 'Put this belt around your waist and buckle them on to it.' At the last moment Hilary grabbed her fold-up fishing-kit-in-a-case and an aluminum pie plate, which was the only cooking container light enough to carry. Finally they slipped down the back stairs and outside.

'Going on an expedition?' called Mother, as they went by. 'I thought you wanted to swim!'

'We do,' said Yop coolly. 'We're going into the woods, too.' He lowered his voice. 'Now, keep calm,' he warned the others, as they set off across the lawn. 'Don't let on . . . Let's not spoil things at the last minute.'

And Hilary, the reluctant participant, thought, It's funny, but I couldn't spoil things if I wanted to. I've just *got* to go along.

Mother was well aware of the atmosphere at supper, but she was sensible enough to recognise a force greater than her own. If she stopped the children, they would certainly try to sneak out later, and anyway, what could she say? That they seemed too eager to go out, so they should stay in? 'Oh, God,' she prayed silently, as she watched them cross the lawn, 'protect them, if they need it . . . What can I do? Should I follow them?'

Her worried thoughts were interrupted by the doorbell. It was Joe Harris, musical instrument in hand as always. He wanted to do a little more work this evening, so that he could go away tomorrow with some friends.

'Of course, Joe,' she said distractedly, 'but you needn't have bothered . . .' She suddenly had an idea. 'Could you do something else for me, though? The children are up to something – I really don't know what. If you could keep an eye on them without them knowing you're watching . . . I hate to spy on them, but I'm worried . . . They've gone toward the woods.'

'Certainly,' he answered, and in a flash, in fact almost before Mother realized what was happening, Joe had disappeared around the house and into the garden. When she looked out of the window a minute later there was no one to be seen.

Anxious thoughts jolted one another in Hilary's head as she followed the others through the woods. I don't want to go into that slimy pond . . . Oh, I wish I knew if we were doing the right thing. What if we drown? Poor Mum! But it can't be more than two or three feet deep. And we can all swim. But where can he be taking us? What if we can't get back again?

All Phyllis's concentration was centred on the frog, who was waiting in a state of semi-torpor at the edge of the pond. He was much smaller again, and for a few seconds she had to look around desperately to find him.

'At last!' he warbled, and with a momentous effort blew himself up to an immense size. He grabbed a hand each, of Phyllis and Yop. 'All hold hands, and in we go!' he sang, and waddled forward unsteadily on his hind feet.

Yop reached for Hilary and squeezed her hand reassuringly. They edged their way down through the water and slime. Hilary shivered and shut her eyes. Such was their absorption that no one noticed Joe hurrying through the trees.

'Now, down we go!' ordered the frog. 'You'll have to hold your breath for a little while. Don't let go, and we'll be up again in no time.' He ploughed into the

13

pond, and the three children suddenly found themselves pulled under by an enormous whirling force. Hilary reached up her free hand as if in a hopeless attempt to grasp the world she was leaving. And that world grasped her, in the person of Joe the gardener, who, willy-nilly, was pulled under too.

3
The Great Pond

'Swim for your lives!' shrieked the frog. The chain of hands broke and everyone scrambled to follow, for fear they would be pulled back under by the whirlpool which had transferred them so violently from one world to another. But since the water was only a few feet deep and the burdens they were carrying weighed them down, their feet kept hitting the bottom of the pond. They stood up, breathless and quite shaken, relieved to find themselves in calm water with solid mud underneath.

'That was scary,' said Phyllis. 'I'm still dizzy. I thought we would be whirled and whirled until we drowned!'

Hilary nodded in profound agreement, letting out an enormous sigh of relief that they had actually arrived somewhere.

They were in the middle of a large lake hundreds of times the size of the pond they had just left. Before them was a vast expanse of calm, shining water, with a dark shoreline on the horizon. The sun was low in the sky, and sunset not far off; the colours of sky and water were gently magnificent. The rich, warm air was heavy with the fragrance of pine trees and other less familiar scents.

The frog was swimming toward a thick green mass on the surface of the lake, a few hundred yards away. 'I wonder what he's so jumpy about?' panted Yop, looking with interest at the still water around him. He shrugged, untied the strap which held the tent, and slung it over his shoulder.

'Goodness knows,' said Hilary, refusing to let herself imagine poisonous snakes, crocodiles, piranhas, or any other water danger; or, for that matter, to wonder what it would be like going back. There was simply no point in being anything but calm and controlled. 'I suppose we'd better follow him.' She turned to rescue the aluminium plate which had slipped from under her belt and floated behind her, and saw something which cheered her enormously.

'Joe!' she cried. 'Was it you that grabbed my hand?' The gardener was not all that much older than they were, perhaps, but what a comfort it was to see him standing there in his red shirt and frayed shorts, tanned, familiar and strong!

'Joe!' echoed Yop. 'How did you get here?'

'I-I hardly know.' Joe reddened, as if embarrassed at intruding on their adventure. 'I saw Hilary go under, thought she was drowning, and when I took her hand I was pulled along, too!'

'And I bet you're wondering where you are!' exclaimed Phyllis.

'As we all are,' said Hilary. 'All we know is, this is called the Great Pond, and we're here in the mud to help out a frog.'

'It may be muddy, Hilary, but it's a lot cleaner than our little pond. In fact, it's beautiful!' said Yop. 'And look, there's an island right behind us. It's going to be great to explore here!'

'I can see why he calls it the Great Pond,' admitted Hilary gruffly. Dark blue and shimmering gold-blue in the water, pink and purple and red in the sky; entirely the place to lose yourself in the splendours of nature. But maybe that green, friendly-looking island was the one harbouring a thief! She glanced at Yop, and realized that he was wondering much the same thing.

The frog, who had by this time noticed that he was alone, was swimming back towards them, beckoning and warbling. Phyllis took Joe's hand. 'I'm glad you're here,' she said. 'Come and meet our friend the frog.' In an excited whisper she added, 'He can talk!'

The amphibian, however, when he had seen Joe, showed no interest in polite formalities. His eyes were bulging out, his purple spots were pulsing, and he turned back somersaults from sheer agitation.

'Who is this? Who is this?' he babbled hysterically.

Phyllis hastened to explain. 'It's all right. He's just our gardener. He came along by accident, but he'll be a great help, I'm sure.'

'But an adult human!' shuddered the frog. 'At best they ignore us, and at the worst they eat us. And he might try to take you back! Even your elder sister didn't want you to come.'

'That's not fair,' retorted Phyllis. 'She just needed a little time to get used to the idea. She's only trying to take proper care of me. She would never hurt anyone, and neither would Joe.'

Yop thought wryly of the time only last year when he and his cousins had tried frogs' legs at a French restaurant.

Joe smiled gravely. 'Well, I won't eat you, and I'm certainly in no position to ignore you.' He added, in a formal manner which conveyed both dignity and reassurance, 'I am Joe Harris, a gardener and musician. I have only the best of intentions toward you and your kind.'

'Musician! Well, well . . . I could never turn a musician away.' The frog drew himself up with great pride, and announced, 'I am Man, a director of the Froggy Choir.' He spoke with such confidence that any comments which rose to their lips, about Man being a strange name for a frog, were immediately stifled.

'Which reminds me,' said Yop. 'What do we do now?'

'Let me explain to you where we are,' declared Man. 'This –' he swept an arm in a majestic half-circle – 'this is the Great Pond.' He paused so that the significance of his statement could sink in. His voice was filled with love and reverence. 'This is our pondly environment. It is here that we sing our songs.'

The frog's tone made Yop a little uncomfortable; he wasn't sure why. It was too meaningful, too heavy somehow. 'This is a wonderful place!' he said vigorously.

Hilary smiled in sudden amusement, reflecting that Yop was always uneasy when life became too serious. For the first time she felt a surge of real sympathy for the frog. If the mandolin was so important to him – if it was somehow part of what she had just sensed in his voice – then perhaps it *had* been the right decision to come here to help get it back. A measure of relief, mingled with a strange exhilaration, passed through her.

'What's that?' asked Phyllis, pointing to the green mass towards which Man had been swimming earlier.

'That is the stage where most of the performances are held. And back there –' they all turned with the motion of his hand – 'is the Maidenfrog's Island. You can't see it because of the other island in front of it, where the treacherous human thief is holding the mandolin!'

The thief's island was an ordinary-looking island, with rocks, sand, and a mixed forest with plenty of pines. It was close behind them in the direction from which they had come. To their left the island rose steeply to form cliffs, and to the right it sloped down to a low shore.

'It looks so uninhabited,' said Yop, 'except for frogs, of course.' He looked apologetically at Man. 'Are there human beings anywhere near, except for the thief? Where did he come from?'

'All around the Pond,' said Man, 'are the swamps. The humans live on the far side of them. Not many people come here, because of the insects and the dangers of the swamps, but sometimes a persistent one or two will get through. What they want here, I'll never understand. There are many other ponds to explore; why do they have to choose this one? Usually, we notice them and keep out of their way, but it disrupts our practices and throws the froggy concerts completely off schedule.

'Once a group of students came here to study the environment, which I suppose is a worthy occupation. But they stayed and stayed, and to make things even worse, they had a dog who was an absolute menace. A few children whom they had brought along actually spoke to us, and tried to control the dog, but it was no use, and eventually we became so desperate that we stopped eating mosquitoes and flies, and the large numbers of insects drove the humans away.'

'I bet you had a feast when they left,' sparkled Phyllis.

'Indeed we did! But now – when I think that the thief got through, right on to the Maiden's Island, without being seen, it makes me shudder – and I know why it happened! We were so wrapped up in our music, in the Maidenfrog and the mandolin, that we simply weren't watching as we should.' He sighed, a miserable, throaty sigh.

'What did he do? Just grab it from your Maidenfrog?'

'Oh, heavens, no! He didn't see her at all, I hope!' Man turned pale green at the thought. 'She left it on a rock in the clearing, after practising, and when one of the handmaidenfrogs went to fetch it she found the thief' his eyes closed in pain at the thought – '*playing it*! How dared he touch our sacred mandolin!

'She raised the alarm, and every available frog rushed to recover the mandolin. We were afraid he would fight us, but the Maidenfrog cried from within the forest, 'Don't hurt my frogs!' Immediately, he turned and ran, taking the mandolin with him. We chased him across to the other island, but he is much faster on land than we are, and soon disappeared into the woods.

'Our first move was to hide his boat, so he couldn't escape that way. Then we tried to creep up on him during the night – just to take the mandolin. We meant him no harm. But he was holding the mandolin even in his sleep, and he woke up and got away again.

'Our next idea was to reason with him, but every time a frog approached, he started throwing rockets! He never came close to hitting anyone, so I suppose he was respecting the Maidenfrog's plea; but who knows whether he'll continue to be so careful, if he feels he has no choice?

'We all met this afternoon to try to find another way to get the mandolin back. Our next concert is in only a few days! After hours of useless discussion, I gave up and came to your world, hoping to find children as understanding as the ones we had met in the past. At first I thought it was a terrible misfortune to fall into your pool, but how lucky I was to be rescued by such noble, wonderful humans as you!'

After a mildly embarrassed pause, Phyllis asked, 'Why is it so important to have your concert on time?'

Man sighed again. 'We were created to sing. Harmony is our goal in life. All winter we sleep, to build up our strength, and in summer we sing. We have to sing! Autumn will soon be here, and we must expend all our strength in singing before then. What worse fate is there than *not* to do what you were created for?'

There seemed to be no answer to this. Silence hung like a motionless bell over the little group. What worse fate indeed? Hilary felt, but hardly realized that she was feeling, as if a door had been unlocked inside her and was ready to swing wide at the slightest push. Then Yop spoke, and the sensation passed away.

'We'd better get down to business,' he said. 'Should we go there –?'

But before Yop could finish his question, the tranquillity of the pond was shattered. From the island came a loud bang, followed by a red flare and a rain of multicoloured sparks high over the cliffs. The frog shrieked in terror. 'Rockets!' he yelped, and swam as

21

fast as his legs would take him, away from the island toward the stage.

'Hey! Wait!' cried Phyllis, and hurried after him.

'Forget the frog! Let's catch the thief!' Yop plunged joyfully toward the island.

'No, stop!' shouted Joe. He caught up with Yop and grabbed him by the arm.

Yop wriggled angrily. 'Let me go! What's the matter with you? Let's go and catch the thief!'

'The way you're going,' said Joe severely, 'will only bring you right back home again! You're heading directly to the spot we came from!'

'Oh.' Yop reddened. 'Maybe you're right. Although how you can know exactly where . . .'

'I took my bearings when we came up,' said Joe. 'We surfaced right below that muddy slope over there.'

'Anyway, we don't want to take chances,' shuddered Hilary, and then decided not to say anything more. Yop was looking both annoyed and embarrassed, and was no doubt upset at not having thought of taking bearings himself.

'It's probably too late to catch him now,' he said bitterly.

'We'll have other chances,' Hilary said mildly. Seeing Yop upset and Joe uncomfortable strengthened her resolve to be reasonable and calm. Yop might be clever and brave, but at eleven years old he was three years younger than her and still a child. Perhaps, she hoped, Joe would understand that. 'Wasn't it a beautiful firework? We'll have to tell the frogs not to be afraid. Did you see all the colours?'

'I'm beginning to get fed up with this stupid frog, always panicking about silly things,' said Yop. 'He's so jumpy!'

'That's the natural way for a frog to be,' grinned Joe.

Yop chuckled back, his good humour returning. 'Let's go and see where he's trying to take us. But I'm going back to that island the first chance I get!'

4

Complications

As she approached the stage Phyllis saw that it was a massive network of lilypads, with a white flower snaking through here and there to break the expanse of green. The effect was quite charming, and at first Phyllis stood still and stared, absorbing the multitude of sights and sounds, glad that the others were still a long way behind her.

Several frogs at the front of the stage were involved in a heated discussion, and behind them, adding to the chaotic effect, a whole horde of others were making funny, discordant noises rather like the tuning-up of an orchestra. Now and then one of them would pause, flick out his tongue, and gobble a passing insect.

They were all bigger than frogs in our world, though not as big as Man had been when he took Phyllis and the others through the whirlpool. Man, at what she supposed was his regular size, was very much a medium frog amongst the others. Much as Man had changed his size at will by the side of the pool, the frogs in the choir breathed in enormous amounts of air, blowing their whole bodies up like balloons before letting it out in musical sounds.

24

Complications

The frogs came in all shades of green and grey, some with coloured spots and some without. The colours were in constant, flickering movement, and the spots of those involved in the argument pulsed in and out, perhaps in time with their emotions. Watching them seemed to drown her eyes and ears in sensation.

Gradually, though, the meaning of their argument began to dawn on Phyllis. The frogs wanted Man to keep the humans away from the stage; in fact, they wished he hadn't brought them to the Great Pond at all!

'Look!' shouted a big deep-green and grey bullfrog with a loud voice. 'Look, Man, here's one of them already, eavesdropping on us. That's a human for you – no sense of shame!'

Phyllis turned red. 'But– but! –'

The big frog glowered at her and continued even louder than before, 'And the others are not so far behind. Now what are you going to do to stop them?' He towered accusingly over Phyllis's little friend. 'Do you realize the risk you're taking?'

'Yes, Duke, I do,' yelped Man. 'In a situation like this risks have to be taken. And rules have to be broken.'

'But these are sacred rules,' said a red-spotted frog in hushed, humbly-rumbly tones. 'These humans don't belong here. We can't sing with intruders around!'

'They won't be listening to us sing, Andu, they'll be getting the mandolin back for us. And what use are sacred rules anyway, if they defeat their own purpose? Two days – only two days until the next concert. We need the Maidenfrog and her mandolin. These children are honourable creatures. They braved the whirlpool, and will keep their promise to help us.'

'And the other one, the adult? Don't!' Duke waved an arm impatiently as Man tried to speak. 'Don't tell me again that he's a musician. Nonsense! Even if he *is* a musician – and we only have his word for that – he's just another human. What if they become friendly with the thief? I say we should send them home. Then we have only one wicked person to deal with.'

'And how do you mean to deal with him?' argued Man. 'Are you going to fight? Isn't that against the sacred rules, too?'

'Perhaps we should resign ourselves to losing the mandolin,' offered a limp-looking yellow and green frog. 'We could ask for another one . . . but it would take some time to get it, and it would be so embarrassing . . .'

'Oh, Uka, no!' came several cries of genuine anguish. 'We need it *now*!'

A silver-spotted frog with long grey whiskers came slowly forward. 'Hush, hush!' he said gently. 'You too,' he said to the choir in the background. 'I want you all to hear what I have to say.

'Let's try once more to look at this situation sensibly. Man shouldn't have invited these humans without our consent – I'm not trying to excuse him – but now that they are here we mustn't become hysterical.'

'Quite right,' answered Andu. 'What we need is *order*. If we stick by the sacred rules all will be well.'

Both Man and Duke opened their mouths to protest, but Andu quelled them with an upraised hand. 'Let Kas speak. He is the oldest and wisest, and deserves our respect.'

'Oh, all right,' muttered Duke. He squatted back and kept a wary eye on Phyllis. Man turned his worried face to Kas, who was silent for at least a minute before he spoke.

'Why do we have sacred rules?' asked Kas finally.

'To guide us,' replied Man.

'Exactly!' Duke interrupted. 'They guide us to keep away from humans!'

'Be quiet, Duke!' said Andu. 'But you're quite right,' he added smugly.

'And for protection,' continued Man in a low voice.

'Yes! From humans!' crowed Duke triumphantly, jumping up and down.

'And from fighting!' retorted Man passionately. 'And from wasting our time doing things that don't help us to progress! If we follow the sacred rules we sing the most wonderful songs in the greatest of harmony. You know that from experience! Our pond becomes a paradise . . .' He stopped, choked with emotion, tears pouring down his face. 'But if the rules are preventing that harmony –'

'How dare you profane the sacred rules!' gasped Andu, stiff and pale with anger.

'Here are the rest of the humans, butting in on our councils,' stormed Duke. He sneered horribly at the surprised faces of Yop, Hilary and Joe, who had just reached the platform. Then he turned to Kas and growled, 'Well, what do *you* suggest?'

Kas waited calmly for a few seconds and then asked, very softly, 'Have the sacred rules ever been changed? Do they always remain the same?'

For a few moments there was complete silence. Then all the frogs began to shout and shriek. 'That was different! That was right, but this time it's wrong! We're not ready for any changes! We have to keep our Pond the same!' The ugly babbling swelled and rose into a chant repeated over and over, 'Humans are treacherous, stupid and mean! Humans are treacherous, stupid and mean!'

Then, suddenly, the chanting fell to a murmur and died away, and the frogs looked at each other uncomfortably, as if they had all had the same thought at once.

Andu shuddered. 'What a regrettable lapse from good manners,' he said.

'And our purpose is to create harmony?' queried Uka sarcastically.

'There, you see,' said Kas, quick to take advantage of their shame. 'Here's where you're making a mistake. Maybe it's time for changes, maybe not. I don't know. But it *is* time to think a little about humans. What proof do you have that they are mean? Hmm?' He looked around challengingly.

'There was one student,' said Andu bitterly, 'who threw a spear at us for fun!'

'One student out of many,' pleaded Man. 'And didn't the others get him to stop?'

'Some of them were eating frogs,' said Uka blandly. 'None of us, of course, only non-talking ones, but I don't call that right.'

'They didn't know any better,' said Kas. 'They eat a lot of dumb animals the way we eat insects. How were they to know about talking frogs?' He paused. 'They are often thoughtless, no doubt, and blind to what's around them. So are we frogs at times. But why do you call them treacherous? Have we ever entered into any dealings with them?'

'Of course not!' chorused the frogs.

'Then how could they have been treacherous? Treachery is a breaking of faith —'

'But – but –' Duke began to turn purple with fury, because Kas was making so much sense. 'They would be treacherous if they had the chance!'

'Fiddlesticks!' said Kas. 'You have no proof! And you call them stupid when they show every sign of high intelligence. I won't go into details now –' He stopped and looked meaningfully at the other frogs. 'But, frankly, we have more proof of the good qualities of humans than of the bad. It seems to me that we will gradually have to rid ourselves of our prejudices against humans, and get used to them –'

'Never, never!' moaned the frogs. 'Impossible!'

Duke started jumping up and down with agitation. 'You must be mad. You know what's at stake – a lot more than a mandolin and some sacred rules. You know what we have to lose! I tell you, it's just not safe having these people around. Let's drive them away!' He turned, his greyish spots pulsing like bubbles in a pool of boiling mud, and made a horrible raspberry noise directly at the four humans.

Phyllis screamed, and they all recoiled at the ugly green spray that landed on them. They dipped their faces in the water and washed it off, in shock and disgust.

The rest of the frogs were as upset as the humans. 'Oh, Duke,' uttered the sacred-minded Andu, his voice filled with pain. 'Oh, Duke, please don't!' He collected himself and faced the humans with dignity. 'I'm so sorry. Please accept our apologies for him. The majority feeling is that it's best if you humans return to your own environment. We appreciate your kind offer to help, but we can't accept it. Thank you.'

He bowed, and pointedly turned to the Froggy Choir behind him. The others turned away too, except Kas, who sat wearily rubbing his head, and poor miserable Man.

Man slumped over the lilypads, his head down in despair, shame and confusion. The humans stood quietly waiting, feeling helpless and somewhat indignant at the welcome they had received.

'M-man,' ventured Phyllis, going closer and reaching out a tentative hand to touch his head. Her eyes filled with tears.

Man looked up, to reveal that he was crying, too. His tears flowed out one after the other, big and iridescent, purple and green, shining in the sunset. Splash! Splash! They fell with heart-breaking regularity into the pond and dispersed in gleaming ripples.

'I'll take you back,' he said, his voice brimming with distress. He shook the tears away and dived abruptly past them toward the island.

There was nothing to do but follow.

The four humans stood close to the shore, facing the frog and the island. 'We're not going,' said Phyllis.

Man's eyes bulged out to their fullest extent. 'But –' He looked in amazement at the four serious faces.

'No, we mean it,' said Joe. 'We'll stay at least a day or two to see if we can help. Unless, of course, you agree with the others that we should return home.'

'Oh, no,' replied Man. 'I think you should stay. But how can I be sure when almost everyone disagrees with me?' Another tear spilled over, and he bobbed his head into the water and blew his nose.

'But the silvery one is on your side!' said Phyllis eagerly.

'Yes, Kas always looks at things calmly and reasonably. He is old now, and is much more patient with the others than I. But I don't like to talk about sides. We frogs can't take sides against each other. How can we make music if there is no harmony amongst us?'

'Won't you have a lot of trouble with the other frogs if we stay?' asked Hilary. 'Are you quite sure it's worth it?'

'Maybe you could stay here with us,' suggested Phyllis.

'No, no, thank you, but I must go back and try to make peace with my brother frogs.'

'Tell them we promise not to listen in on their choir practices,' said Yop.

'Why, thank you!' said Man. 'How considerate of you!' He hesitated, looking uncomfortable. 'You have another friend here, my sister Jonquil, who is one of the handmaidenfrogs on the Maiden's Island. However, she may not be able to approach you, and you *must not* try to contact her. There is one promise you must make me if you are to stay here. Please – please do not cross the land bridge to the Maiden's Island. I am a rule-breaker, no doubt, but that is one rule that must not be broken.' He looked at them expectantly, and they all agreed. 'I'll be back whenever I can.'

And with that, Man was gone.

5
Another Firework

Yop lay awake on the space blanket, far into the night. Joe Harris was sprawled peacefully at the other side of the blanket, and the two girls were in the tent. Fortunately it was too warm to need covers, and the starry sky held no threat of rain.

There had been quite a dispute over who was to sleep where. The argument had gone on the whole time they were putting up the tent. Joe Harris had insisted on sleeping outside, on the grounds that he was older than they were, he was used to sleeping in the open (or so he said), and it was their tent anyway.

Yop had automatically assumed that he, as the other male, would sleep on the space blanket with Joe, but Hilary had been quite annoyingly stubborn. Why should she and Phyllis be treated differently because they were girls? she demanded. Then suddenly, as they finished pitching the tent, she had fallen silent, and Yop thought he knew why. Luckily, the abrupt descent of darkness saved the situation. Phyllis might be brave as a lion in the daytime, but at night it was another story.

'Please, Hilary,' said Phyllis, 'please sleep with me

in the tent. I don't want to sleep outside anyway, and
you know I need you to talk to if I wake up scared of
the dark.'

Phyllis had sounded so tired, and so much like her
little sister again, that Hilary was able to give in
gracefully. She hung the bathing suits over a tree
limb, folded the knapsacks up for pillows, and joined
Phyllis in deep, exhausted sleep.

Yop stared up at the stars, breathing deeply,
absorbing the atmosphere of this strange new world.
But was it really so strange? The night sky, for
example. He couldn't see any of the familiar constel-
lations, but somehow, all the same, it looked like the
sky at home. Some of the vegetation, such as pine
trees and lilypads, was also found in his own world.
The night sounds, too, were much like what he was
used to; crickets singing perhaps a higher note, frogs
– were they the same talking frogs? – croaking around
the pond. The place seemed like another version of
home, if that was possible; another way of saying the
same thing . . .

He turned his mind to other matters, and tried to
sort out all that had happened that evening. Two
major questions occupied his thoughts. First of all,
why had the thief run off with the mandolin, and why
was he so stubborn about keeping it? Perhaps he ran
for fear of the frogs, thought Yop. They might be
frightening if they came at you in a noisy, hysterical
horde. But then why didn't he just drop the mandolin?
Or, if he had instinctively held on to the mandolin as
he ran, why didn't he leave it in an obvious place
afterwards, so that the frogs could find it?

It looked as if the thief definitely wanted to keep
the mandolin. He even held it while he slept, and

scared the frogs away every time they came near! But why? For the frogs it seemed to be merely a musical instrument vital to their songs; but it must have some other value for the thief to want it so badly. Was it made of gold, perhaps, or studded with rubies? Or did it possess magical powers?

Yop grinned and shook himself. 'This isn't "Jack and the Beanstalk",' he said to the sleeping Joe and the night at large. 'It's just another world, and I've always believed *that* was possible.'

The other question concerned the attitude of the frogs. Why were they so set on getting rid of the humans? It couldn't be just to keep them away from their concerts. Come to think of it, Duke, just before that awful raspberry, had said there was a lot more at stake than a mandolin and some sacred rules.

Now, the mandolin was enormously important to the frogs. Before Yop had arrived at the stage, one of the frogs had been talking about getting a new mandolin. Phyllis had told him about the heartfelt cry of the other frogs: 'We need it right *now*!' Man had said that losing the mandolin would keep them from doing what they were created for. What could be worse?

And yet for most of the frogs, having the humans at the Great Pond was even more of a catastrophe. They were ready to give up a chance of getting the mandolin back, just to keep people away. It didn't make sense! Yop was on the threshold of sleep when an idea jerked him wide awake again.

The Maiden's Island! Yop was willing to bet anything that it was because of much more than a sacred rule that Man had made them give their word not to go there. What treasures might the frogs have hidden there? He finally fell asleep trying to think of a way to get to the Maiden's Island without breaking his promise.

In her dream Hilary was a frog, a beautiful frog with red garlands around her head and long curly hair which flew behind her as she ran. But frogs don't run, they hop; so she hopped, and then ran again, and chased the thief, crying. 'Don't drop my mandolin, you'll break my heart! . . . my mandolin, my mandolin, my heart!'

Whap!

Hilary sat up and stared into the darkness. No, it wasn't her mandolin or her heart that had been broken, but what was that noise that had woken her up? She listened, trying not to let her imagination overcome her. Why hadn't they thought of setting up a watch during the night?

A light wind had arisen, making the air less sticky and hot but the atmosphere far more spooky. Hilary reached out for the comforting warmth of Phyllis lying beside her. There was a sudden gust of wind, and another whap!

'Ouch!' said Joe Harris. Then there was a long silence.

I will not sound hysterical, said Hilary to herself. 'What happened, Joe?' she asked in her calmest voice.

'It was a nut! It fell off the tree and landed on my head! Ooh, that hurts!'

'Well, at least it wasn't the thief attacking us!'

Joe laughed. 'Don't worry. I'm sleeping with one ear open. Good-night.'

'Good-night.'

*

When Yop opened his eyes again it was daylight. He woke abruptly, filled with happy anticipation of the day ahead. Rapturous, chaotic birdsong filled the air; chirps, twitters, full-bodied whistles and squawks. Yop stood up and stretched. The air smelled fresh and clear, and a light breeze made it a tiny bit cool. The sky was still pale, almost white, but held the promise of a deep blue, burning day.

Joe was nowhere in sight. Yop peeked into the tent; his cousins were still fast asleep. He walked down to the shore and looked along it to left and right. There was nothing but sand, rocks and trees, and a few water birds hopping about in the shallows. The great pond stretched ahead of him, blue and silver in the early morning. He could see the stage, but it was too far away to tell if there was any movement there.

Was Joe already looking for the thief? Yop considered skirting around the end of the island, but decided instead to go up through the forest towards the other side of the island. That way he would be covering new ground, and also could more easily keep out of sight.

As he plunged into the edge of the forest, brambles grabbed his legs and arms, and he just stopped himself from exclaiming in pain. As he detached his scratched limbs from the thorns he noticed that the brambles were blackberry canes loaded with ripe fruit. Delighted, he picked and ate a handful before pressing on.

Cautiously he made his way up through the trees. It was slow going, for there was plenty of undergrowth, and it took more control or skill than Yop possessed to go silently through the woods. How had the Indians managed it, he wondered, and resolved to practise a softer walk when he was back home again.

The climb was a steep one, and there was a no sign of life except for more birds and a squirrel which ran up a tree long before he came near. After about ten minutes Yop stopped for a breather. His stomach, stimulated by the blackberries, started to grumble, and he wished he had thought of bringing a yoghurt bar. He went through all his knowledge of wilderness foods. Various berries, roots, wild garlic and onions, pine tea . . . Hadn't he read something about pine tea being bad for cattle? Was it harmful for people, too?

Much of the vegetation was only vaguely familiar, so he could not be sure whether he had seen the same plants before, or only similar ones. He saw many hickory trees, but their nuts, which had startled Hilary during the night, were still unripe. And ferns, but it was too late for fiddleheads. What, apart from blackberries, were they going to eat in this place?

Bang! It was the sound of another firecracker, back toward the whirlpool end of the island. Then came a series of strange yelps. Yop forgot about his empty stomach and headed toward the noise. Every sense alert, his heart pounding with excitement, he crept through the forest. Presently he heard someone coming through the woods, and slid behind a tree.

The sound was coming from the opposite direction, up on the hill, away from the firecracker! Puzzled, he peered around the tree. What a disappointment! Joe came jogging easily through the undergrowth, his red shirt like a beacon.

'Joe, did you see him?' whispered Yop.

'No, did you?'

Yop shook his head. 'How can we possibly surprise

37

him if you make all that noise coming through the woods, and wear a red shirt, of all things! It's too bad you haven't got that camouflage suit, the one you wore the first day you came to our house.'

Joe looked rueful. 'You're right. Actually, I was just looking around to see if I could find some food. Then crack! that firework went off. I rather thought the thief might come and talk to us if he saw us. But that's two fireworks now since we came – so it looks as if he wants to keep us away, too.'

'How can he think we're scared of fireworks!' snorted Yop. 'He must be somewhere between here and the end of the island. You go up and I'll go down. And don't forget to look up in the trees. Maybe he'll climb one to hide.'

Impatiently, Yop watched Joe disappear, more quietly this time, into the woods. Then he set off, all his muscles tensed to avoid betraying himself by the slightest noise. But he saw and heard nothing but more birds. When he reached the steep slope leading down to the lake shore, he was hardly surprised to find no sign of the thief. There was only the slightest ripple on the Great Pond, only the faintest rustle of the breeze in the trees.

Yop threw up his hands in bafflement and turned to follow the bare rock up the edge of the forest. Joe was kicking around in the dirt, about a hundred yards above him. They soon met midway.

'Where could the thief have gone?' demanded Yop. 'I thought we had him trapped!'

'Maybe he went over the cliffs,' shrugged Joe. He held out the remains of a firecracker. 'Not very powerful, but enough to scare a frog. Did you hear that funny shrieking sound just after it went off? Man made the same sort of sound yesterday.'

Sure enough, not far out in the pond were the heads of several frogs, raised just above the surface. Big googly eyes stared unblinkingly at Yop and Joe. Hastily they stepped back into the woods.

'I wonder how Man is doing,' said Joe. 'Those frogs certainly look hostile.'

Yop's mind was still on the thief. 'He didn't go down to the beach, that's clear.'

'Man? What are you talking about?'

'Tch! No, the thief, of course. If he'd gone down there, those silly frogs would be long gone, or making a huge rumpus. Did you look to see if there was a way down the cliffs?'

'It looked like a sheer drop to me,' said Joe.

'He's vanished into thin air,' said Yop. 'We've got to find a way to catch him! Oh, let's go and have breakfast! Who can make plans on an empty stomach?'

6
A Strange Fish

'It doesn't make sense!' said Hilary, in dismay. 'We were just supposed to go to the thief and talk to him, not chase all over the island trying to find him! It could take forever!' She handed out four yoghurt bars and hacked the remaining two into halves. 'We don't have time for plans and strategies, and being clever. We have to go home!'

'You can go back if you want to,' said Yop.

'Don't be silly,' said Hilary crossly. 'I'm responsible for Phyllis, and besides, I *want* to help. I'm just worried that Man may be wrong, and days and days will have gone by when we get home. Poor Mother!'

Joe looked at Hilary, concern in his friendly eyes. 'I wish I could reassure you,' he said. 'But really, I don't think you should be anxious. I can't tell you how I know, but I'm quite sure everything's all right.'

'Thank you,' said Hilary, looking a little brighter. She took a deep breath and focused her mind on practical matters. 'This is all the food we have, except for blackberries. You go ahead and plan what you like. I'm going fishing for our lunch. And Phyllis wants to stay near the camp in case Man comes back.'

'I have to go over that whole area where Joe and I were this morning,' said Yop. 'There must be a hiding place somewhere. I still can't believe it! He's just disappeared!'

Joe grinned. 'What if we split the island in two? You can have that end, and I'll try the other. While we look for the thief we can keep an eye open for wild foods. I saw some mint plants this morning . . .' A smile flickered across his face. 'By the way, what do you plan to do if you *find* the thief?'

'Talk to him. And fight, if I have to,' shrugged Yop. He paused reflectively. 'Gosh, I hadn't thought of that. Fighting won't be any use if he's much bigger than me!'

'I don't think Man will like it if we fight,' said Phyllis. 'He said fighting was against their sacred rules.'

'Why don't we make flags of truce?' suggested Hilary. 'Who knows,' she said hopefully, 'if he sees that we're peaceful, maybe he'll want to come out and talk to us!'

Hilary picked her way slowly along the shore. Their tent was pitched on a sandy strip of beach not far from the whirlpool end of the island, and they had been lucky to find such a good place at dusk the previous evening. The sandy area ended not long past the camp, so she left Phyllis there to swim and watch for Man. A flag of truce, made of a long stick and Phyllis's white T-shirt, was planted in the sand; Yop had made a smaller flag of truce with his own white shorts, and was carrying it through the woods.

'I'm going to fish off those rocks down there,' said

Hilary to her sister. 'Stay here. You'll scare the fish away if you splash around near me.'

She found a comfortable rock and cast her line. The float lay lazily on the surface of the water, and Hilary found herself drinking in the atmosphere of the wilderness with such a pang of pleasure that she almost cried. The trees, the water, the deepening blue of the sky were like a reflection of a long-awaited camping trip in her own world. Suddenly Hilary remembered how much she liked fishing. Cheer up, stupid, she said to herself. Aren't you always dying to go fishing, when we're at home?

It was peaceful and pleasant, reeling in her line, casting, watching the float for that telltale bobbing. But the fish weren't interested. She found herself staring restlessly at the low shoreline across the water, probably not many miles away, wondering how far the swamp stretched, and from what kind of place and from how far away the thief had come. After an hour she had caught just one little fish. Normally she would have thrown him back in, but now she felt obliged to hang on to anything that might just be edible.

Phyllis came wading along the water's edge with a collection of gleaming stones she had found. 'I'm going to save them and take them home, if I can find something to carry them in.'

'They won't look half as pretty when they're dry.'

'Spoilsport! I'll make a tray with them, and varnish them.'

'You'll need flat stones for that.'

That should keep her busy for a while, thought Hilary, as Phyllis wandered back down the beach. The day was quickly becoming very hot, and there seemed to be less and less chance of catching any fish. She reeled in her line and went farther up the shore toward the Maiden's Island, looking for a cooler spot. Presently she found a fallen tree half in the shallows of the pond, with many of its roots worn smooth in contorted, almost sculptured shapes. The forest grew close to the shoreline here, shading a large patch of water. She cast again and sat looking at the Maiden's Island.

Only a small portion of the Maiden's Island was visible, jutting out from behind the shore of their own island. It didn't look at all unusual, but Hilary couldn't help feeling curious after being told so pointedly to keep away. Perhaps she would have better luck fishing from the Maiden's Island . . .

She had caught a few more small fish, trout this time, when a much larger fish jumped out of the water and landed on the fallen tree beside her. Hilary started, and almost let go of her rod. Instead of flipping itself back into the pond, the fish stayed quite comfortably on the tree and looked at her. Its eyes bulged out and moved around almost as if on stalks, in the most unnerving way. What a strange fish!

At least, she supposed it was a fish. It looked like one, but also it reminded her somewhat of a tadpole, and its face was a little like a frog's. In the place of a ventral fin was a sort of sucker which held it quite securely on the log. Because of its movable eyes, she couldn't tell for certain when it was looking at her, and when it was looking up at the sky, or the water, or at a few insects which it casually snapped up from the fallen tree. In spite of its strangeness, however, Hilary was sure, although she didn't know why, that the fish was friendly.

'Hello, hello, hello!' it gurgled finally, in a cheerful voice. 'We seem to be having more than our accustomed share of humans these days. My name is Gobi Peri Socrates. What's yours?'

'Hilary.'

'Well, Hilary! Welcome to the Great Pond. And who's that down the beach?'

'That's my sister Phyllis.' Hilary looked anxiously at her rod and the small pile of dead fish. 'I didn't know there were talking fish here. I hope I haven't caught anything I shouldn't!'

'Of course not. No talking fish is foolish enough to get caught. I assume you have no talking fish in your world.'

'No,' said Hilary, and then added, 'At least, not that I'm aware of. After this experience – coming to your world, seeing the frogs and now you – I'm not sure *what* I know.'

The fish laughed. 'That's a healthy attitude. It shows you've already started doing what you came here for.'

'What do you mean? We came here to help the frogs get their mandolin!'

'Certainly, but you in particular must be here to learn something, as well. Otherwise you wouldn't be talking to me!'

'Oh! . . .' said Hilary, and then stopped, not knowing quite what to say next.

Gobi Peri Socrates chuckled understandingly, and gulped down another insect. Then he unfolded long fins, rather like arms, from his sides, picked a leaf from an overhanging branch, and hopped over to one of the dead tree's roots. Holding the leaf in one fin, he started vigorously rubbing the root. His mobile eyes trained themselves forcefully ahead, as if all their energy, usually spent in movement, was concentrated on the job to be done.

'I am a sculptor,' he said. 'Feel free to fish while I work. And think hard. You have things to talk about and questions to ask me in the short time you are here.'

Hilary cast her line. What was this strange fish talking about? How could she possibly have come here to learn something? She frowned in Gobi's direction, suspicion and anticipation chasing each other back and forth through her mind. This must be some kind of joke, she said to herself, and instantly answered, no, it's not, and you have to work out what it *is*.

After a while Phyllis came up carrying a plastic bag full of stones, and was introduced to the industrious fish. By this time Hilary, with a startling change of luck, had quickly caught several more trout. 'It's crazy!' she said. 'The weather's getting hotter and the fish are biting better!'

'The best fishing,' said Gobi Peri Socrates, 'is from the Maiden's Island at a cooler time of day. But I suppose the frogs have forbidden you to go there.'

Hilary and Phyllis nodded.

'How silly of them!' he exclaimed. 'It will never work. Don't take them too seriously. They don't know what's good for them.'

'But we really mustn't go to the Maiden's Island, even to fish,' said Hilary. 'We promised to stay away.'

'That's fine! Keep your promise, and if it's meant to be broken it will break itself quite nicely. Of course, it would be much simpler if the frogs would use their brains a little. They're such emotional creatures! Thinking farther ahead than the next song is so new to them that it completely mixes them up.'

45

This forthright speech seemed to Hilary to sum things up rather well, and maybe to explain a few things besides, but Phyllis was immediately on the defensive. She glared at Gobi Peri Socrates and said in as polite a voice as she could muster, 'Excuse me, please; I don't want to be rude, but who are you to say the frogs don't know what they're doing? How do we know that *you* know what you're talking about?'

'Why, by my name, of course – Socrates. That means I'm very wise. And Peri – which is for my eyes. Haven't you noticed? I can look every way at once; so I can see my way clearly around any problem!'

'And what does Gobi mean?' asked Hilary.

'It's after the Gobi Desert, because I can survive on dry land for a while, unlike other fish.'

'That's certainly true,' admitted Hilary.

The fish chuckled. 'Also, I've been told all my life, 'Go be wise, go be wise', so now I *am* Gobi-Wise!'

'But still, Man is such a nice frog,' protested Phyllis. 'Actually, I *know* he isn't mixed up. *He* was the one who came to get us, and he knows that we only want to help. I think he's very clever!'

Gobi grinned. Have you ever seen a fish grin? 'What a lovely, loyal girl you are! And you're quite right; Man, and a few others, are no doubt the best of the frogs: the pioneers of progress, you might say. But even Man doesn't understand quite what is happening, or where it will lead. Your being here will help him out. Whew!'

He jumped back into the pond and swam about for a few minutes, his eyes at one moment under the water, and at the next popping out. Soon he leapt back to the log, took another leaf, and started rubbing once more. 'My throat and fins were dry, with all that talking and all this work,' he explained.

Hilary continued fishing, musing over what Gobi had said. The problem in the Great Pond seemed to be much more than a stolen mandolin, and who knew how long it would take to sort things out? And now it seemed that she had a purpose of her own here, whatever it was. Oh dear, she thought, wondering about her mother again. I'm afraid I'll have to go back home just for a few minutes, to see if everything's all right. It won't be fun going through that whirlpool, but I may have no choice.

Two more fish took the lure one after the other, and Hilary began to wonder vaguely if Gobi was bringing her luck. She sat staring into the water, trying to gather her wandering thoughts. Then an exclamation from Phyllis made her turn her head.

'Look! When he polishes the wood it turns to gold!'

Under the seeming magic of Gobi's fins, the wood was changing shape, and colour too. In some places it shone gold and gleaming. For the first time, Hilary noticed that the root on which Gobi Peri Socrates was working was somewhat gourd-shaped, with a short neck coming out of it. Almost before she had time to guess, Gobi said casually, 'I'm making a new mandolin for the frogs. It hasn't quite taken shape yet, but it won't be long now.'

Phyllis faltered, 'You don't think we'll get their mandolin back from them?'

'I didn't say that. But it's time to make a new one.'

'Says who?'

'No one says so. It's simply time.'

'You just know that it's time?' asked Phyllis sarcastically. 'More of your wisdom?'

'That's right,' said the fish with composure, and laughed. He seemed quite unoffended by her scepticism.

'I'm no expert, but I don't think it looks quite like what we call a mandolin,' commented Hilary. 'More like a fat guitar, maybe.'

'This is not quite like the first one,' said Gobi. 'It's a little bigger, and a little rounder, but it's constructed on much the same principles.'

The gold of the wood, where he was no longer polishing it, was beginning to fade slightly. 'It has to be polished before every concert,' Gobi commented. 'The golden colour blends with its golden sound.'

'I'm sure I've seen wood like that before,' said Hilary. 'Unpolished, that is, not golden.'

'No doubt you have,' said Gobi. 'The gold can be brought out only by rubbing it with its own leaves.'

Hilary gathered up her fish. She was getting hungry, and these should be enough for lunch. A thought came to her. 'Do you know if there's any other food here that we could eat? Can you tell us where, and what to look for?'

'Yes, there is food, but unfortunately I mustn't interfere. Ask Man. You're his guests; he has to help you. And just watch,' he chortled, 'just watch how he reacts when you tell him about the new mandolin! The frogs were incredibly silly when we made the first one in the spring; and now they can't do without it! Goodbye!'

He wiggled his eyes and plunged into the water. Just as Hilary was thinking unhappily that she needed more time to talk to Gobi, and wondering if she would see him again, he reappeared at the surface.

'Wait,' he cried, 'I have a message for you, Hilary. "Don't worry, it's all right!"'

'For me? From whom?'

'I don't know,' said Gobi. 'It's not given to me to know from whom. I just get the message and pass it on. It's like knowing when to make a mandolin.'

'Oh,' said Hilary, digesting this. 'What's the message?'

'I just told you. It's, "Don't worry, it's all right!" '

'Oh, thank you!' For some strange reason relief filled her whole being. 'Thank you very much!'

'You're very welcome. See you later!' said Gobi Peri Socrates, and swam away.

7
Discoveries and Angry Frogs

Yop spent a frustrating morning with his mind divided between edible plants and the mandolin thief. He combed his half of the island with the utmost care, looking behind every rock and into every tree stump and hollow. There was no sign of the thief, and to make matters worse, not one edible plant, as far as Yop knew.

And that, exactly, was his other problem; he didn't know enough about edible wild plants to recognize them even if he saw them. How stupid can I get? he thought. I got that plant book for my birthday, and just looked through it in a hurry! He made a promise to himself to read it carefully, find the plants, and try eating them, once he got home, but what use was that now?

By the time he reached the whirlpool end of the island, Yop felt that the whole morning had been wasted. It was then that he made the first of two discoveries that saved the day.

After glancing dejectedly at the tranquil water and the deserted stage, he turned up toward the cliffs, hoping perhaps Joe had failed to notice a way down

them. Along the edge of the forest were more blackberries, and Yop picked and ate a few. He was walking
on bare rock now. Would there be lichen here? He
looked carefully at the rock; nothing. Just as well, as
he had no idea which lichens were edible.

But the rock, after all, was not quite bare. What
was that whitish-grey, powdery substance, smudged
mostly, but sometimes, on top of the smears, in a short
even line on the rock? He rubbed some with his fingers.
It looked so familiar! Now and then, there were black,
burnt-looking spots. He turned back down the island,
to see where the trail of powder began. Soon the traces
became completely smudged and spread out, often
much wider than before, and led all the way to the
muddy area above the whirlpool. He followed the trail
back up the island, and around the corner to the top
of the cliffs. There it ended, at another burnt spot.

Was it ashes from a fuse? That would explain how
the thief had set off a firecracker when he was nowhere
near it. Yop wished he knew for certain whether a
fuse ended up as ashes, or just as burnt string. He
sighed. His confidence in his own general knowledge
was being knocked out of him, blow by blow. And even
if he had all that knowledge, what was true in his own
world might not be true in this one!

But this was no time to get discouraged. Supposing
the powder *was* ashes, why was it spread about on the
rock, largely so up here, and completely farther down?
Even if he and Joe had walked over it, unnoticing,
their steps couldn't have made so many smudges. It
would have taken several trips up and down the rock
to accidentally wipe out so much of the line of ashes.
It must have been done on purpose. Two firecrackers,
thought Yop, and two fuses; the first fuse a very long

one, leading from the whirlpool area all the way to the top of the cliffs, where the firework had gone off last night. The thief had had plenty of time to clean up after that. And the second, shorter fuse from the top of the cliffs, where it had been lit, to the spot where Joe had picked up the firework this morning. But couldn't the thief have spread *those* ashes thoroughly, too, while they were having breakfast?

And back to the old question, where had he gone, after he had set off the firecracker? Yop lay down on his stomach at the edge of the cliff, with his head hanging over. Just as Joe had said, there was no way down; only a ragged wall of stone with a few plants pushing out of the crannies here and there, rocks and lake below, and definitely no hiding place.

The only way he could have gone, then, was back towards where Yop and Joe had come from when they first heard the firecracker that morning. Yop shrugged. It was distinctly possible that the thief had avoided Joe amongst the trees. After all, Joe hadn't even been watching for him!

Yop stood up and looked around. The cliffs offered a panoramic view of the Great Pond. There were other islands too far away for anything moving on them to be seen, but he could tell they were forested like this one. Land, even more indistinct, or perhaps it was swamp, lay all around the pond.

The sun was now high in the bright sky, and Yop was beginning to feel hot and thirsty. The fastest way to that cool, inviting water was no doubt by going back along the end of the island and past the whirlpool, but what an uninteresting course to take! Yop decided to forget about thieves and plants for a while, and indulge in some good, healthy exploration. Looking along the top of the cliffs, it didn't appear to be such a very long way before he would be able to climb down to the shore; and maybe he would catch a glimpse of the mysterious Maiden's Island before returning to camp.

He followed the long slope quickly and without incident. The cliffs eventually ended in a jumble of huge rocks with trees and shrubs growing from between them. There was no doubt in Yop's mind that he could find a way through them, but it might be long and tedious. The grassy verge ahead looked much more promising. He continued forward, and after only a short while it widened into a meadow which reached to the end of the island.

At last, an edible plant that he knew! Wild onions! Not very filling, perhaps, but they would taste wonderful with the fish Hilary was certain to catch. He dug up several with his jackknife.

The best was yet to come. Down at the end of the island were two peach trees, loaded with fruit. Behind them was a natural bridge joining their island to a smaller one, which must be the Maiden's Island. There were more peach trees on the smaller island. What a find!

The peaches were ripe and delicious. He devoured one and then another, and decided to finish off his snack with an onion. He slid sideways down a steep bank to the water's edge close by the land bridge, to drink some water and peel and rinse one of the onions. He had just finished, and was looking speculatively at the Maiden's Island, when the angry head of Duke the frog popped out of the water before him.

'Bllllhhhhoooo!' A green raspberry spray was directed right at Yop's face. He fell back, dripping and disgusted, and his onion floated away into the pond. He spat furiously, wiping his face with the back of his arm. The spray made him feel sick, and a horrible anger surged inside him.

Duke blew himself up to enormous proportions, his spots pulsating violently. 'Go away! Get out of here!' he yelled, his foghorn voice sharpened by desperation, and poised himself to spit again.

'Oh, shut up! Go away yourself, you green creep!' Yop advanced toward the frog, fists clenched. Duke backed away, deflating rapidly, shaking with anger and fear.

Yop stopped abruptly, feeling silly and ashamed. I can't hit this poor stupid frog, he thought. What's the matter with me?

'I'm not going to hurt you,' he said. 'But don't spray me again. Let me wash this yucky stuff off.' He splashed his face with water, and then his arms and chest, feeling extremely thankful that he had removed his shirt earlier and tied it to the flag of truce. 'What did you do that for?' he demanded, trying to sound composed and reasonable, but still looking frightening to Duke. It was easier to wash off the frog spit than an angry frown.

'Because I want you to go away!' sputtered Duke. 'Why are you staying here? And what are you doing so close to the Maidenfrog's Island? Man said you promised to keep off!'

'I have kept off it. I'm just getting some peaches to eat. And you made me lose my onion!'

'You wouldn't need to look for food if you had gone home as we told you to,' said Duke. 'I'm glad you lost your onion!'

'Oh, don't be so silly, Duke!' said another voice, and

54

Andu, the frog who had been so cold and formal over at the stage, appeared. He was accompanied by Uka, yellow-spotted and listless as before.

'Here is your onion,' said Andu. 'I apologize once again, that Duke was so rude. But he's right. Why can't you leave us alone?'

'But we're here to help you!'

'We don't need your help,' said Andu. 'Besides, I think you're here more to satisfy your own curiosity than to help us. You're just an adventurer.'

Yop had to admit, at least to himself, that this was largely true. However, Phyllis was there with the purest of motives, and Hilary only because of a reluctant courage.

'But I don't mean any harm,' he protested.

'Then go away,' said Andu, 'and you'll be sure to *do* none. We'll get the mandolin back by ourselves.'

'I bet you won't,' said Yop. 'We haven't even seen the person who took it. He's very crafty.'

'Typical of a human,' sighed Uka.

Duke, who had regained his courage, started to chant in a militant voice:

> Humans are wicked, humans are mean,
> But we can keep the Great Pond clean!
> Humans are ugly, noisy and wrong!
> But we can keep the joy in our song!

'Hush!' said Andu. 'That childish drivel is forbidden now. We don't want to offend –' He broke off suddenly.

'Oh, don't worry about me,' said Yop. 'He can't do worse than he's aleady done!'

'We're not worried about offending *you*,' sneered Duke. 'Besides, Andu, we've added a few more lines:

> Thanks to the insects, the swamps and the fear,

Only the purest of the pure dwells here!

Duke filled his enormous throat with air and burst into an ecstatic refrain:

We love the Maidenfrog! The Maidenfrog!–

All at once he stopped, deflated, and became quite purple with confusion. 'Sorry,' he whispered, looking unhappily at Andu.

A spasm of annoyance passed across Andu's knobbly features, and his red spots flickered slightly. Without even looking at Duke, he said to Yop, 'Go, just go! You said you can't find the thief. That shows how useless you are. You don't belong here. So please – just leave!'

He dived into the pond. Uka followed slowly, after extinguishing his yellow lights one by one in a way that would have seemed sinister if he had not been a frog. Duke glared sullenly at Yop and prepared to let off another raspberry spray.

Yop laughed and retreated a little to be out of range. 'Don't bother,' he said. I don't like being spat at, but it won't stop me. It just makes me more determined to stay.'

'Keep away from the Maiden's Island or I'll – I'll –!' Duke looked as if he was about to burst into tears. He shook his head fiercely, plunged furiously, helplessly into the water, and was gone.

Yop stood gazing thoughtfully after the frogs, feeling a little regretful about what he had said. That look of despair on Duke's face . . . What could he be so terribly upset about? And what had he done that was so wrong? He had only sung that they loved the Maidenfrog! What was the matter with that? Was it only that wicked humans weren't supposed to hear the frogs sing, or was it something else?

Yop was thinking over the whole incident when he was startled by Joe coming up behind him, holding several sprigs of wild mint. 'This is all I found,' he said. 'I saw you talking to more frogs. What did they have to say for themselves?'

'That horrible one called Duke spat all over me,' said Yop. 'Yuck! They're like a bunch of fanatics about keeping people away, especially from the Maiden's Island.' He glanced across at the tranquil, ordinary-looking little island. 'I wonder what's so important about it?'

'Probably nothing, for us,' said Joe. 'But they're worried and scared, obviously, so I think we should respect their wishes and keep off.' He picked a peach and bit into it. 'These are wonderful, Yop! What luck to find them!'

'That's why I came down here – only to pick peaches. I didn't try to go to the Maiden's Island. And I was only down near that little bridge of land because I had to wash an onion –'

'I understand,' insisted Joe in a grave voice, 'but I think we should stay away as much as possible. Poor things, we don't want them more frightened than they already are!'

There are few things worse than being preached at, especially when you have already reached the same conclusion on your own. Yop had to turn away and start picking peaches, so as not to show his temper. He removed his shirt from the flag of truce, laid it on the ground, and began to cover it with fruit. It was the closest thing he had to a bag.

'Good idea,' said Joe heartily, following suit. 'If we can carry enough home, we won't have to come back often.' He paused, but Yop was still silent. 'By the way, I've found a clue to the whereabouts of our missing thief!'

'What? Where?'

'There's a hollow tree a little way into the woods, about a hundred yards from the cliff side of the island. In it I found firecrackers, matches, a frying pan, a spatula, and a small tin of lard. Considering that he has all that cooking apparatus, it's surprising we've seen no sign of a fire.'

'Maybe he has nothing to cook. He can't fish with everyone after him. Why didn't you take the stuff?'

'We want the thief, not his cooking utensils,' said Joe reasonably. 'I was careful not to disturb anything, and I hope he won't notice that anyone was there. If we keep a close watch on the tree, maybe we'll catch him!'

'Hmmm . . . There wasn't anything else in the tree?' asked Yop slowly. 'Only cooking things, and firecrackers and matches?'

Joe shook his head. 'Why?'

'I just wondered,' said Yop vaguely, shrugging his shoulders. But his thoughts were far from vague, and Joe had an unusually quiet companion as they followed the shore back to camp.

8
Lunchtime

'What was that all about?' asked Phyllis. 'What did he mean, 'Don't worry, it's all right'?

'I can't be sure,' said Hilary, 'but I think it means I shouldn't worry about Mother.'

'But that doesn't make sense! Are you going to listen to a message from nowhere, given to you by that weird fish? Not that there's anything to worry about, but I don't think much of Gobi. He's so conceited!'

'I thought he was just straightforward,' said Hilary. 'Anyway, his message made me feel a lot better.' She stood still and looked helplessly at her sister. 'I don't understand why, Phyllis, but I feel so completely relieved . . .'

'Humph!' said Phyllis, and stumped on down the beach.

While Hilary gutted the fish, Phyllis made a fire. She gathered a pile of dry wood, twigs and dead leaves, breaking the bigger sticks across her bare knees. She formed a ring of smallish stones and put a few larger stones inside, on which to balance the aluminum plate. Soon there was a steady blaze crackling amid the stones, and Hilary was able to start cooking the fish.

Hilary put the first two fish on the plate with a little water, so that she wouldn't burn or boil the fish. The plastic container was beside her, full of water to be added as needed. It was a full-time occupation, trying to keep the plate balanced on the stones, and to maintain just the right amount of water. She had to take the plate right off the fire to turn the fish, using the tent's carrying bag as a potholder.

What were they to use as plates? The choice was between the torn wrappers from the yoghurt bars and plastic bags! And they would have to eat with their fingers, when the fish were cool enough. She took the plate off the fire and removed the trout with the knife and hatchet. Setting them carefully on the stones at the edge of the fire, she put another two on the plate. Then she sat back with satisfaction, thinking how good their lunch would be, and how pleasant this world of the Great Pond really was.

'Hurrah for the girls!'

The delightful smell of fish, mingled with wood smoke, roused Yop from his thoughts. He loped ahead of Joe towards the tantalizing odour. 'Look what we've brought – peaches and wild onions! And mint! We can put some of the onions in with the fish. How many did you catch?'

'Two trout each. And one little one – but I don't know if it's edible.'

'Great,' said Yop. He opened his improvised sack, and the two girls pounced on the peaches.

'Oh, I was so hungry,' slurped Hilary, the juice running down her chin. Hastily she wiped it away and turned to Joe. 'Hi! We've some interesting things to tell you! Where did you find the peaches?'

'Yop found them at that end of the island,' pointed Joe. 'And he met some more angry frogs there. But let's eat before we talk. I'm ravenous.'

Yop went to the shore to wash the onions, once again feeling irritated at Joe. But why? Joe had just given him credit where it was due. Maybe it was Hilary's obvious dependence on Joe. Perhaps Joe *should* be the leader, so to speak, because he was the eldest, but Yop simply didn't feel comfortable about it. After all, I hardly know him, he thought; he's only been our gardener for a few weeks. And why should we need a leader anyway, and why should Hilary want someone to depend on? She was usually too cautious, but perfectly able to take care of herself, and Yop liked her that way. He shrugged, dismissing these uncomfortable feelings, and tried to concentrate on the business in hand.

Phyllis had already launched into a bitter description of Gobi Peri Socrates. 'Hilary liked him,' she said, 'but I thought he was just awful! . . .'

Hilary, making a wry face at Joe, offered a trout each to him and Yop. Phyllis wouldn't be ready to eat until she had unburdened herself. Hilary turned over the fish on the plate, added water and the clean onions Yop handed her, and sat back to watch her sister let off steam.

'And I don't know *what* to think now,' said Phyllis. 'I don't know what to believe and what not to believe, and whether or not to tell Man about the new mandolin!'

'Calm down,' said Joe, giving her a quick, reassuring hug. 'We'll sort it all out.' He winked at Hilary. 'This fish character doesn't seem to have thrown *you* into confusion.'

'No, not at all,' answered Hilary, her face lightly flushed. 'I found him terribly comforting. Everything he said sounded just right to me.'

'Are you sure the new mandolin isn't simply a replacement?' asked Joe.

'Gobi didn't say it was. What he seemed to be saying was that just because he was making a new one it didn't mean that we wouldn't find the old one.'

'So we have to keep looking for the thief,' said Yop. 'Good. I don't want to leave until I find him, and I want to know what's on the Maiden's Island, too. Why shouldn't we just go there? Didn't your Gobi say they were being silly, and that the Maiden's Island was the best place to fish?'

'He also said we should keep our promise,' said Hilary. 'I'm going to wait, and if I'm supposed to find out what's there, it'll just happen. Anyway, I think they only want to keep the Maidenfrog hidden. They probably think we're not worthy to see her. Maybe there's a sacred rule about it.'

'Not pure enough,' said Yop. 'Duke said, "Only the purest of the pure dwells here." Well, I told him all his putting-off tactics make me even more curious.'

'Oh, you shouldn't have!' exclaimed Joe. 'That will make them even worse. And just when it's time to break the news about the new mandolin!'

'Oh, do we *have* to?' groaned Phyllis. 'I don't want to get them upset!'

'But don't you realize what this means?' said Joe, looking more excited than Yop had ever seen him. 'At worst the old mandolin is gone, and there will be a new one. But if the new one isn't a replacement, it must be for another player!'

'Another Maidenfrog?' suggested Phyllis.

'Or a Frogman,' chuckled Yop.

'They already have one of those,' said Hilary. 'Listen, do you suppose Man is trying to hog the limelight, and that's worrying the other frogs?'

'He wouldn't,' said Phyllis firmly. 'He's not like that.'

'Gobi said the frogs would be upset when they heard about the new mandolin,' said Hilary. 'But if the old one is gone for good they should be happy to get another; and if it's for another player, wouldn't two mandolins be better than one?'

'Two heads are,' murmured Yop idiotically, 'two hearts beating as one . . .'

'Oh, stop being so silly,' giggled Phyllis, and then noticed that Joe had gone very red in the face. 'What's wrong? You're blushing!'

'No, I'm not,' said Joe, jumping up. 'I'm hot, that's all. Who's for a swim before we get back to work?'

'Maybe Joe has a romantic temperament and a girlfriend to encourage it,' teased Yop. 'But I bet he doesn't read romantic books like you, Hilary.'

'I don't read them very often,' scowled Hilary.

By this time Joe had recovered his colour and composure. 'How do you know about "two hearts beating as one"?' he asked Yop. 'You must have been reading romances, too!'

'Just research,' answered Yop. 'I want to find out about everything, and even that rubbish needed a little investigation.'

'Oh, yes?' said Joe sarcastically. 'Let's get back to

some real investigation. I think, for this afternoon, we should have another go at finding the thief-'

'I'll watch by the tree,' broke in Yop, who had an investigation all of his own to pursue. 'Tell the girls what you found there!'

'If you don't find the thief by suppertime, please let's borrow his cooking things,' said Hilary, after Joe had explained. 'It would be so much easier to cook with a real frying pan! Even the littlest fish was good, but think how much better it would be fried in fat. Oh!' A look of chagrin came over her face. 'I forgot. I'm no good at frying. I always burn things.'

'I'll cook the fish,' said Joe. 'I'm an expert on campfire frying, and any other frying, for that matter. You catch 'em, I'll cook 'em!'

'Great!' said Hilary. 'We could put a note in the tree, explaining, and telling him we just want to talk to him. Maybe the smell of good food will tempt him to join us. Gosh! I wonder what he has to eat? Poor man, he can't fish or light a fire, or we'll find him!'

'Maybe he has food hidden somewhere. And come to think of it, I bet he has a hiding place for the mandolin, too. I can't believe he carries it around with him all the time. I wish I knew why he *wants* the mandolin,' said Yop.

'The only idea that occurs to me,' said Joe, 'is that he's a musician, and wants to play it.'

'Then why doesn't he make friends with the frogs, instead of shooting firecrackers? You saw how Man accepted you when you said you were a musician.'

'True, but Man was the only one who accepted me. Can you imagine the others lending their precious mandolin to a human?'

'I wonder if it would be difficult to play an instrument made for frogs,' pondered Hilary. 'It must be different from what we're used to.' She shrugged. 'Well, I'm going fishing. Fish are all the food we have, until we see Man again.'

'I know what my job is,' sighed Phyllis.

Hilary set off for her afternoon's fishing with a feeling of exhilaration, leaving an anxious Phyllis in the camp to wait for Man. 'Cheer up,' said Hilary. 'I have a feeling that everything's going to be fine!'

But why am I so certain that things will work out? Hilary asked herself as she wandered down the beach. It doesn't make sense – Phyllis is quite right – but that doesn't seem to matter. I don't know why, but I *believe* Gobi. And I feel so sure now that we were right to come to this world, but why couldn't I have sensed that before we came?

She put this question to Gobi when she finally met him working on the mandolin again. It had been strangely difficult to find him; somehow she seemed unable to find the spot where they had met before. Her fishing was fairly successful, however, and she was just considering going back to the camp when Gobi called to her from only a short distance away.

'This is all so exciting and special and – and magic, somehow, Gobi,' she said, overjoyed to see him again. 'And I'm sure it's the most important thing that's ever happened to me. But what if I had decided not to come to the Great Pond? Just imagining not having come here gives me the shivers. When something is so important, shouldn't it be easier to know what to do?'

Gobi stopped working and stared at her. His eyes seemed to stick out on their stalks even more than ever. 'Easy? You think magic, as you call it, can come easily? Ha!' He flipped back to the edge of the water and glared measuringly at the new mandolin.

Hilary reddened. 'I know it sounds silly, but when you imagine a magical experience, if you know what I mean, it seems so easy and natural, and – and – as if it was *meant*, somehow. But this whole thing, right from the start, has been so hard!'

'But natural, and as if it was meant to happen!'

'Oh, yes!' exclaimed Hilary. 'I just never expected –'

'Real life, and I mean *real* life,' said Gobi, returning to work, 'has its moments of pleasure and its rewards, but it's always hard. The really magical experiences have to be earned!'

After a few more minutes' vigorous labour he leapt abruptly into the pond. '*I* have earned a few moments' rest – but only a few, because the mandolin has to be finished by tomorrow. And *you* have only a short time left here with a lot to learn, so hop to it!'

He swam away, leaving Hilary open-mouthed and wondering what on earth she was supposed to do now.

9
Frogs in Misery

Phyllis felt lonely and restless, waiting in the camp for Man. What if he can't come this afternoon, she thought; and even if he does turn up, what will I say to him? I don't want to make him even more upset than he already is!

It was hot sitting in the sun, and after a while she decided to cool down by wading out to the stage, keeping an eye on the camp at the same time.

The stage was completely bare, and looked very forlorn. Even the white flowers seemed about to wilt. That may have been because of the heat of the day, but it made Phyllis feel quite empty inside. She stood looking around, a little uncomfortable about intruding on a sacred place, and feeling reluctant to climb on to the stage for a better view. It felt even more lonely there than at the camp, and after a few minutes she turned back toward the shore. She had taken only a few strides when she heard voices rising up in bubbles from the pond.

The first voice broke the surface on a groan. 'How can I know, Kas, how can I know?'

That was definitely Man, but where was he?

'You have to be reasonable,' said Kas. 'I know your heart is breaking, but you can't let yourself be drowned by your emotions. What's done is done. You have to look at what has happened, decide what's right and wrong, and go forward.'

'But I don't know what's right and wrong, and –' Man's voice disappeared in a mass of noisy bubbles. The sounds were coming from the far side of the stage, and Phyllis waded hesitantly toward them.

'Pull yourself together!' snapped Kas. 'You have an excellent sense of right and wrong!'

'But everyone's against me,' moaned Man.

'I'm not,' said Kas.

'I know,' said Man, 'and that helps, but even though I have confidence in you, I have to be satisfied within myself . . .'

'Quite right, of course you do. But you won't get there if you don't use your head. Now think! Do you feel it's right to keep *all* humans away?'

'No, no! Of course not! Well, just look at –!'

Kas chuckled. 'Exactly. Now. We both know that the sacred rules have been changed in the past. Doesn't it make sense, then, that the rules may be altered again in the future, depending on circumstances?'

'Yes, but they won't be changed by me!' Man wailed. 'I'm so frightened! What if I'm doing harm? I don't want to be the cause of disharmony and misery, but I know, I *know* that many humans are good!'

'It takes two to cause disunity,' said Kas firmly. 'The others are being unreasonable, and we both know it. We've done our best. If the rules are to be changed, it won't be by you or me; we don't have that kind of responsibility. All we have to do is recognize the change when it comes, and have the courage to go through with it. What an exciting prospect that is!'

'But what will happen *now*? Oh help, please help!' prayed Man despairingly, and flapped up on to the stage.

'Man! There you are!' exclaimed Phyllis. 'I heard your voices, but I couldn't see you . . .'

'We were largely under water,' said Kas, leaping up beside Man. 'Well, child, here we are, and in great difficulties.'

Phyllis looked from one frog to the other. They looked quite desperately tired; Man's face was full of pain and misery, and Kas's too, but with more resignation, perhaps because of his age.

'What's wrong?' quivered Phyllis.

'It's all over,' said Man. 'There will be no concert tomorrow night. The harmony of the Froggy Choir is gone!'

'They won't talk to us,' said Kas. 'They won't even practise in the hope that some understanding may be reached.'

'Then we should leave,' said Phyllis. 'Maybe if we're gone you can get back together again. Wouldn't it be better to have a choir without a mandolin, than no choir at all?'

'It's no use,' said Man. 'I was at the point of giving up, after hours of pleading and explaining. I didn't know any more whether I had done right or wrong, and had admitted as much, when Uka said, "Even if you change your mind now, it's too late. How can we ever trust you again?"' His head dropped in hopelessness.

'We've come here to sing a mourning song,' said Kas. They started wailing in unison, swaying back and forth. Yop would have found it hard not to laugh at the strange sight, but Phyllis found herself blinking back tears.

'Where have they all gone?' she asked, when finally they paused for a second or two.

'They are setting up positions of defence around the Maiden's Island, especially near the natural bridge connecting it to your island. They will fight to the death, if necessary.'

'But why do they think we'll attack them? We don't want to go the Maiden's Island. Well, that's not really true. We can't help but be curious. But I for one won't go there if you tell me not to. And we would *never* hurt the frogs.'

'Thank you, kind Phyllis,' said Man. 'If there is any human I would trust to go there, it is you. But you must not – just in case, by some miracle, all is not lost!'

Phyllis jumped up, beaming all over. 'But all is not lost! It can't be! I have news for you, and I thought it was bad news, but now I think it might be good! Gobi Socrates said you would be upset when you heard it, but I'm sure you won't be.'

'You've been talking to Gobi-Wise, have you?' murmured Kas. 'I suppose he told you how silly we frogs are, and can you blame him? Look at the mess we're in. His speaking to you is a privilege. He never appears to anyone unworthy.'

'Actually, it was my sister Hilary he came to,' confessed Phyllis. 'I was there, but I was angry at him for being rude about you frogs.'

'What's the news?' asked Man impatiently.

'Gobi is making a new mandolin!' Phyllis looked apprehensively at the two frogs, who sat as if transfixed, their spots pulsing and flickering. That's one hurdle over, she thought, and I don't have to worry about the other things Gobi said. If the frogs don't mind, how can I object? 'Gobi said you were among the best of the frogs, Man,' she added, as the amphibians remained silent. 'And that you and a few others were held back by the rest.'

Tears sprang into Man's eyes. 'I am honoured,' he said simply.

A slow smile was spreading over Kas's face. 'Do you realize what this means? It can't be the end of the choir. Gobi-Wise would make a new mandolin only if it was to be used!'

'That's right,' said Phyllis. 'I told you it was good news.'

Man was still overwhelmed by Gobi's testimonial, but he pulled himself together and said, 'Wonderful news, yes, but it means that the old mandolin is gone for good. You dear humans are free to leave, with our thanks and heartfelt gratitude for your efforts. I'll be sad to see you go, but . . . Shall we find the others?'

'Hold on a minute,' said Kas uneasily. 'That's not the only possibility.'

'What do you mean?'

'Maybe the mandolin is for a new player,' said Phyllis, her eyes sparkling. 'Maybe there will be two!'

Man's eyes boggled out and his mouth dropped open. His purple spots throbbed deeply. He looked completely aghast.

'Did Gobi-Wise say there would be two mandolins?' asked Kas.

'No, not exactly. But when we asked him if that meant we wouldn't get the other mandolin back, he said, "No, I didn't say that." '

'Oh,' groaned Man, gradually slipping lower and lower until his huge chin rested on the stage. 'It can't be possible. We don't have enough harmony for one mandolin, much less two. Do you remember the turmoil, when the Maidenfrog came? . . .' He looked helplessly at Kas.

'Are we in any less turmoil now?'

'But how can we build something new when everything is falling apart?' He lifted his head mournfully. 'It would take a miracle.'

'Wasn't it a miracle when the Maidenfrog came?' demanded Kas. 'Wasn't it a miracle that she survived her illness? It was our love and dedication to her, in spite of our fears, that kept her alive. And how wonderful was our reward!' His eyes widened suddenly, as a realization struck him. 'Don't you see, Man, that this is the confirmation you need? A second mandolin is *proof* that changes are coming!'

'Oh, oh, ooooh,' groaned Man. 'No, I just can't accept that. I don't believe it! But that means I was all wrong . . .' Suddenly he remembered Phyllis's presence, and sat up. 'Oh my, should we be saying all this in front of a human? Excuse me, Phyllis, I don't mean to offend you, but really, Kas, do we have the right?'

'I'm surprised at you, Man!' said Kas. 'When you thought that having humans here was the only way to solve the problem, you were quite willing to trust them!' He paused, as Man flinched and bowed his head, and then continued more gently, 'How long can we keep our secret, Man? Wouldn't it be much easier, and more honourable too, if we could be open and straightforward about it all? In any case, whether you accept it or not, it looks as if at least one more human will have to know everything.'

'Please don't tell me anything you don't want to,' interrupted Phyllis. 'Anyway, I really didn't understand what you were talking about. I don't pick up every single word, like Yop. Oh, I almost forgot. Gobi said you would help us to get food.'

Man's face fell even farther, if that was possible. 'Oh, my,' he said, 'I never thought of that.'

Kas began to laugh.

'What's so funny?' asked Phyllis.

'The food is on the Maiden's Island,' said Kas, quivering all over with mirth.

'Can't you go and get some for us? Oh, the other frogs won't let you. But that's not funny!'

'No, but just think how silly this is. Wouldn't it be simpler if we had nothing to hide, and you could get the food for yourselves?' He laughed and laughed. 'The more we attempt to conceal, the more is revealed!'

Phyllis turned to Man, who was not in the least amused. 'We'll be all right,' she said. 'We can eat fish and fruit, and if the worst comes to the worst, one of us can go back home and sneak some food out.'

'Oh, no, you can't!' Man jumped up and gibbered with alarm. 'If one of you goes back alone, how can you all arrive home only a second after you left? No, don't do that! You can't play that kind of trick on Time. Why, the rest of you might be trapped here for ever, or go back at a quite different time!' He pursed his huge mouth. 'We'll get some food for you.'

Phyllis, who had gone quite pale at the thought of what might have happened, said, 'But you mustn't get hurt because of us.'

'They won't hurt us,' said Kas. 'But I'd rather not be seen, because it will mean more angry words. We'll manage it somehow.'

'Oh dear,' said Phyllis, not at all convinced. 'We seem to be more trouble than we're worth.' Suddenly, thinking of their delicious lunch, she felt ashamed of herself and her companions. 'Please, I mean it!' she said. 'We don't really need any more food. We had a great breakfast and lunch, and although it's not what we're used to, it's quite good enough. I'm not even hungry now, and it's ages since we ate.'

But the frogs would not change their minds. 'How can we invite you here,' Man demanded fiercely, 'and not give you the best we have to offer?'

10
A Brush with Time

After Man and Kas had gone Phyllis sat worrying about them, and feeling rather bitter against the other frogs. Why wouldn't they even try to co-operate? Couldn't they sense that Man and Kas meant well?

She started wading vaguely in the direction of the whirlpool, hoping she might meet some of the frogs who had been swimming there this morning. Maybe she could talk to them.

Keeping well out from the shore so as to avoid a disastrous trip home, she went back and forth under the baking sun, thinking and looking, but no one was there. Only when she headed towards the shore to the right of the mudbank, planning to rest for a while in the shade, did the frogs appear.

'Aren't you going? Aren't you leaving? We thought you were leaving!' Three little frogs jumped out of the water at her, shrieking.

'You should be going! Jump in, jump in! Go home, go home!'

Phyllis shrieked in return, from shock, backed on to the shore, and let all her thoughts out in a rush.

'I'm not leaving! I'm not going! I came to talk to you.

What's the matter with you all? Why won't you make peace and try to get on? Poor Man and Kas, they're trying so hard to do the right thing. And we're not so bad. In fact, we're quite nice people. We came here to help!'

'She looks nice,' said one frog, swimming closer.

'She behaves nicely . . .' said another, following suit.

'She can't possibly be nice!' said the third, and they all backed away.

'I don't like being unkind,' ventured the second frog.

'Neither do I,' sighed the third.

'But we have no choice!' said the first stoutly. 'For the sake of harmony, we must fight!'

'Oh, come on,' said Phyllis, in complete disgust. 'How can you get harmony by fighting? Besides, it's against your sacred rules. You have to be nice to get harmony. And you have to practise and practise and practise. Man and Kas say you won't even practise!'

'I love practising,' said one frog.

'Me, too. I love singing!' said another.

'Singing with the Maidenfrog! The Maidenfrog! Our joy is strong!' chirped the third, in an amateurish echo of what Duke had sung earlier to Yop.

The others joined in, letting loose their high-pitched voices, practising with all their hearts. Phyllis stood entranced. Then gradually their singing slowed and died away, as one after the other remembered that they should not be performing before a treacherous human. Just like Duke, they had lost themselves in rapturous song and then, unhappily, recollected themselves. It was a very sad moment when the last note died away.

'Oh, dear!' said Phyllis. 'Why couldn't you keep on singing? It was so lovely!'

'Thank you,' said the first frog, touched. 'But we really mustn't.'

'We'd better get back to work,' said the third.

'What work are you doing?'

'We're here to watch, to see if you all go home.'

'Not that it matters,' said the second frog, 'because there won't be any concert.'

'Aah,' moaned the third, 'what will we do if we can't sing? Oh –' He stopped in mid-groan, pointed a finger, and screamed, 'She's a traitor! She's shielding him! The thief! The mandolin!'

The other two frogs yelped, and Phyllis turned, gasping, to see a bush moving up the far side of the muddy bank of the island, above where they had emerged from the whirlpool. The bush was carrying something quite large, covered with slime and mud from the bottom of the pond.

Seized with indignation, Phyllis cried, 'I'm not a traitor! I'll get him!' She splashed through the water and up the near side of the bank, to cut him off. The bush had reached only the top of the slope, not more than twenty yards ahead of her, encumbered as he was by branches and the slimy mandolin. Phyllis rushed across the bank with all her energy, heedless of danger, and slipped – whoosh! – in the mud.

It was a moment of pure terror, an hour in one second, as she slid down towards the water, towards the whirlpool, headed for an accident with Time. She clutched wildly, her fingers digging into the mud, slowing her only a little. Her feet hit the water with a splash; she was up to her knees.

Just at the moment when she knew she was lost, her right hand flung itself out and clutched a low-hanging blackberry cane. She gasped as the thorns dug into her flesh, sending a thousand tiny barbs up her arm. Her hand instinctively pulled back, but the thorns went in even deeper. She was safe for now.

Phyllis gingerly lifted one foot, then the other, dug them into the bank, and took a few deep, shuddering breaths. There was mud in her mouth; she spat; there was mud in her face and hair, but wiping it with her free hand only spread it further.

The only nearby plants were on her right. To get off the mudbank she would have to hold the brambles with her left hand and then let go with the right. She groped for a place on the blackberry stem which was relatively free of prickles, broke off a few, and hung on.

Now to relax her right hand. Her arm and shoulder were aching; her fingers had grown numb in only a few seconds, and seemed to be locked tight. Phyllis pulled up with both arms and found a new foothold. Now, with less weight on her right arm, she was able to relax her fingers and pull them away. Her hand was bleeding, but there was no time to think about that. She flexed her fingers a few times and grabbed another plant, mercifully free of thorns.

When she had finally worked her way to a safe spot Phyllis looked around her, but of course the moving bush was gone. She turned and sat on the bank, giving in to the sobs of pain and frustration.

Two little frogs came up to her carefully, making little comforting noises and looking at her with big sad eyes.

'She's hurt,' said one. 'She's bleeding!'

'She's crying,' said the other, and burst into tears.

'We're so sorry,' mourned the first. 'Let us wash your wounds.' It took her by the fingertips and led her toward the pond. The two amphibians ministered to her wounds, rinsing them gently. They laid her down in the shallows and splashed her all over with cool water, rinsing her muddy hair, bathing her face, and soothing her with cooing, chirping sounds.

'Thank you so much. You're so sweet,' said Phyllis after a while. She sat on the bank and glanced around. 'Where is the other frog? There were three of you!'

'He went after the thief,' answered the frog.

'Across the island?'

'The thief didn't go across the island. He stood up there watching for a few seconds, and then went along to the shore again farther up. One of us went to investigate. Here he comes back!'

Sure enough, the third frog had almost reached them.

'He's going toward the rocks on the other side!' he said breathlessly. 'Oh, please, Miss Human, please follow him and see where he goes. Maybe you can get the mandolin back for us!'

It needed no more to send Phyllis flinging herself up over the rise and then cautiously down the steep rocks on the other side, toward the bottom of the cliffs.

As they watched her go, the three little frogs murmured amongst themselves.

'What a valiant girl!'

'Maybe there *is* more than one good human!'

'Her hands will start bleeding again if she climbs the rocks . . .'

'We must get something for her wounds.'

'From Man and Kas!'

'The healing balm that they used on the Maidenfrog!'

11
Surprise and Suspicion

Yop had finally grown tired of waiting near the tree or prowling around in the vicinity. He had looked carefully through the contents of the hiding place. There were no fuses, and for a while he wondered if perhaps his theory was wrong. But what else could those traces on the rock be? Maybe the thief had hidden the fuses in another place, so that even if the cache was found his disappearing act would remain a secret. But that was no use, if someone else took his fireworks. The only other possibility was that Joe had taken them, and that didn't make sense either.

This brought Yop's train of thought back to his irritation with Joe. First of all, it bothered him to be annoyed; he was used to getting on comfortably with people. Also, he wished he knew Joe better. It was only two weeks since Joe had knocked at the door, a slightly shabby figure with longish hair, dressed in an old top and jeans made of camouflage material, and carrying his guitar. He was looking for gardening work. Auntie Jane, who liked his pleasant air and was tired of trying to keep up with the weeds, had employed him at once.

Everyone soon became comfortable with Joe, who was open and agreeable, and young enough to be a friend; but it takes time to become fully acquainted, and to build up a feeling of confidence and trust. To make things worse, it looked as if Hilary was gradually developing quite a crush on Joe. It won't last, thought Yop suddenly. She'll get bored with it. He's all right, but she has better things to think about.

Staying here is a waste of time, said Yop to himself eventually, and he headed for the cliffs. It was easy to justify his departure. He would have to leave soon anyway, to refill the plastic container with water, which he had taken to sustain him during the long afternoon. And the thief is so clever, he probably already knows I'm here, thought Yop; maybe my leaving will encourage him to come back. I'll keep an ear open.

He came out of the woods just above the rocky area at the end of the cliffs. It was wonderfully uplifting to be in the sunshine again, after the gloom of the forest. He ached to go exploring down those rocks! But he should give the thief a few more minutes, maybe, to return to the hiding place in the woods. Yop scanned the water, but there were no frogs swimming back and forth; in fact, there was no sign of life at all except for a few birds away out on the shore. After a token glance back into the woods, he sat half-hidden by a tree and gave himself up to the pleasure of observing the birds and insects and the shimmering water.

He had been watching for only a few minutes when he saw Phyllis stand up slowly from behind an isolated boulder on the shore, about half-way down the island. He was about to wave and shout to her when he realized that such exposure was hardly wise, and anyway, why was she behaving so strangely? She was looking fixedly at a spot below him, somewhere over to the left; and then all around her, particularly toward the cliffs.

Suddenly, she appeared to notice a pile of branches on the other side of her solitary rock, and picked one up. She stared at it for a few seconds, and then tossed it down. What were those branches doing on the beach at all? wondered Yop. There were no bushes that far down – only mud, rocks, and a few weeds; and they were fresh, green branches, not dead ones blown there in some storm.

After a while, Phyllis left her cover and broke into a slow lope towards him, squelching through the mud or using the rocks as stepping stones. Staying low, she kept on a diagonal course to the cliffs, and soon disappeared beneath them.

The logical conclusion was that she had seen the thief, and was following him. Maybe they could cut him off! How could he signal to her? He cawed twice, vigorously. If anything would let her know he was there, that would. They had been practising bird calls the week before. He could do a bob-white, but the crow was by far the easiest, loudest and most realistic. He hoped that crows existed in the world of the Great Pond.

After waiting a few minutes more, Yop eased his way on to the rocks. He would have to be very careful, because the thief might be hiding down below, or coming up toward him. Before long he could see around the edge of the cliffs. There was Phyllis again, and this time she was facing his way and saw him immediately. She raised a finger to her lips and pointed in the direction in which she had been looking earlier. Yop nodded, and continued slowly down.

The next time he looked at Phyllis, she was just standing, staring, looking completely dazed. What's happening? thought Yop in frustration, craning his neck over the rocks in front of him and seeing nothing. Slowly, as if she had made a decision but wasn't yet sure if it was the right one, Phyllis lowered herself under cover.

After a minute or two of staring at the ground, she raised her hand and looked at Yop, biting her lip in concentration. Then she embarked on a cramped series of gestures and lip movements from behind a rock. Her eyes flickered continuously back to the same spot below Yop.

'You,' she mouthed, pointing at Yop.

'Me?' asked Yop silently. 'What? What should I do?'

'You go down there,' she continued, indicating the area below.

'What about you?'

Phyllis hid behind the rock and then came half-way out again.

'I'll stay here,' mouthed Phyllis, and performed a little pantomime with her fingers. With two fingers of one hand she walked down the rock in front of her, and then stopped as the first hand reached the second, coming up to meet it. Then the two hands walked off together. Finally she pointed to herself, and made two fingers creep out from behind the rock and finish close to where her hands had met.

That seems pretty clear, thought Yop. 'Do I catch him and fight?' he mimed, grabbing an imaginary thief and punching him.

'No!' Shaking her head vehemently, Phyllis walked

her fingers once more down the rock, stopped, smiled, and mouthed, 'Hi!' Then, abruptly, she disappeared into her hiding place again.

Yop stood up, shrugged, and started descending the rocks as quickly as possible. Almost immediately he stubbed his toe and let out a yelp. It ruined any chance of a surprise meeting, but that didn't seem to be the plan in any case.

'Yop!' Joe appeared from behind a bush not far below him, looking quite discomposed.

Yop was flabbergasted, but only for a split second. 'Hi, Joe,' he said jauntily. 'Sorry I deserted my post, but there was no sign of the thief. Have you found anything?'

'Nothing at all,' said Joe. 'I've been searching through these rocks here – I thought maybe the mandolin could be hidden amongst them – but no luck. Do you want to go through that last section with me?' He motioned in the direction of the Maiden's Island. 'After that we could get some more peaches and onions and the frying pan, and go back to camp.'

'Fine,' said Yop immediately. Better to agree and maybe change my mind later, he decided, than to show suspicion now. It seemed incredible, but perhaps he had been feeling uncomfortable about Joe for a good reason!

'You've got some leaves in your hair, Joe. You must have really been searching hard in the woods!' As Joe started forward, ruffling his hair, Yop glanced back to where Phyllis had been. She was watching for him, and immediately raised herself up, gesturing and mouthing, 'Go! Go!' Then she ducked down again and he left reluctantly, trusting and hoping that his younger cousin knew what she was doing.

Phyllis crouched and waited, feeling apprehensive and unhappy but determined, until Yop and Joe had been gone for a while. Most of the time she stared at a certain section of the rocks, identifying and re-identifying it.

When she felt it was safe to move, Phyllis went quickly but quietly to the area under observation. As she approached it she listened carefully, but there was no suspicious sound. Heart thumping, she crept carefully around the last rock.

Just as she had suspected! An opening in the stone, surely too small to shelter a thief, but the perfect place for hiding a mandolin. She slipped her hand in, felt around, and pulled out a globular wooden instrument, somewhat like a guitar, with one long strip of fading gold on the neck. Clutching her treasure, Phyllis climbed down the rocks and returned along the shore from where she had come.

12
Explanations and Complications

Phyllis stood at the edge of the forest and watched the busy camp. She was exhausted and hungry, and longing to unburden herself. But that was exactly what she couldn't do. She would have to hide her secrets and suspicions, just as she had hidden the mandolin, at least until she had had a chance to talk to Yop alone.

The fire was burning merrily, and Joe was cooking potatoes – that was what they looked like! – in the aluminum plate, and fish in a frying pan. It smelled so good that she almost rushed forward to join the others, but then she noticed how absorbed Hilary was in conversation with Joe, how happy she was talking to him, and was overcome with sorrow. Tears sprang to her eyes, and she sat down on the forest floor, desperately trying to control them.

Unaware of the miserable watcher in the woods, Hilary and Joe talked on. Hilary had felt rather shy about discussing her perplexity with Joe. It seemed as if her heart was so full that if she expressed any of its turbulent emotions she would burst somehow, and her whole vulnerable self would be revealed. But she had to talk to someone!

'You don't have to tell me about it if you don't want to, Hilary,' Joe had said, noticing her hesitation. 'I only thought it might help.'

'Oh, I'm sure it will help,' Hilary had answered politely. 'But I – I really don't know where to start.'

'Tell me about Gobi. What's he like?'

That had been easy enough. 'Sounds something like a mud skipper,' said Joe, when Gobi's appearance and habits had been thoroughly described. 'But what is it about him that has upset you so much?'

'It's nothing about *him*!' exclaimed Hilary. 'He's terrific. He's beautifuly blunt and direct, and seems to find everything rather funny. And yet at the same time he's *very* serious, and I can't help but believe everything he says. The problem is –'

Out with it, Hilary, she said to herself. Even if it does sound ridiculous!

'The problem is that he told me that I came here to learn something, not just to help the frogs. And he told me to hop to it! But hop to what?'

There was a long pause. Joe turned the fish carefully, prodded the potatoes, stoked up the fire a little, and then picked up the bunch of mint he had gathered that morning and sat thoughtfully staring at it.

Why doesn't he say something? thought Hilary, fervently wishing she hadn't tried to explain herself, especially to someone (now that she thought about it) she hardly knew.

'What you're saying,' said Joe finally, 'is that he has told you that you're here to learn something, and that you'd better hurry up and do it, but you have no idea what it is. Right?'

'Yes,' said Hilary. 'I know it sounds silly, but –'

'It doesn't sound silly,' said Joe abruptly, picking the mint leaves off the stems and putting them into a neat little pile to make tea with later. 'Actually, it sounds rather frightening – like being tossed into a den of lions and told, "Make friends with them, you can do it!" A sort of do or die situation.'

Gosh, he seems to understand, thought Hilary with relief. Aloud she said, 'That's right, but he seems so cheerful and happy about everything that I feel I'm not supposed to worry! So what do I do? I've thought of asking him directly about what I'm supposed to learn, but I'm absolutely sure he won't give me an answer.'

'Yes, I think you're on your own,' smiled Joe. 'I've never had an experience quite like yours, Hilary, but I'll tell you what I do when I'm stumped. I try to play it by ear- that is, relax and do whatever seems right- and at the same time keep alert for any sign of something new, or different- something I haven't really thought about before. Don't try to force yourself – you'll only get exhausted, and perhaps miss something a relaxed mind might have noticed.'

For a while there was silence except for the brisk sizzling of the fish and an intermittent flick! flick! as Yop, at the water's edge, skimmed stones across the pond.

'Thanks, Joe,' said Hilary finally. 'I think what I have to do is work out what it is about this place that makes me feel so expectant and excited. That's something I don't understand. I've just realized that I felt it as soon as I got here, even before I met Gobi. What he did was make me aware of it.'

'You know what impresses me about this place?' said

Joe. 'It's the incredible sense of purpose of these frogs –'

'Hilary!' called Yop. 'Don't you think I'd better go and look for Phyllis?'

'Yes, I suppose so . . . Where *can* she have got to?'

Now for it, thought Phyllis. She walked resolutely into the camp and said, 'Hi!' as cheerfully as she could.

'Oh, I'm glad you're back!' cried Hilary. 'I was beginning to get worried! We were just thinking of going to look for you. Man told us –'

Phyllis flopped down on the sand and burst into tears. Immediately everyone clustered around her, exclaiming and asking questions, and under cover of wiping her eyes and blowing her nose (for which she was offered the tent bag by Hilary, who said she would rinse it out afterwards), she was able to compose herself.

'Oh, I'm so tired and hungry,' she said, accepting a peach. 'It was a terrible day, except for some sweet little frogs.' She told them of her experiences, first of Man and Kas and their agony, then of the three frogs, the thief, and the muddy slide.

'And you didn't find him?' asked Hilary.

Phyllis winced, and looked down at her wounded hands. This was the moment she had dreaded.

'Of course she didn't,' said Yop immediately. 'She would have told us that first, if she had!'

'Don't feel bad,' said Hilary, noticing a few more tears on her sister's cheeks. Hilary was still feeling rather dismayed and helpless about not knowing what Gobi expected her to do, but she pushed that worry into the back of her mind, determined to cheer up poor Phyllis. 'You've had more success today than anyone.'

If only she knew what's making me sad, thought Phyllis, and felt even sadder.

'Look!' Hilary pointed enthusiastically to the food. 'Man and Kas brought us some potatoes and green beans (we'll eat the beans raw, as salad). They floated them over to us on the neatest little raft of sticks and rushes. The three little frogs went to Man and Kas looking for ointment for you – here it is.' She pulled a tiny wooden pot out of her knapsack. 'And because you were so nice and so brave, they agree with Man now that humans can be all right. You should have seen how happy Man and Kas were to have some friends among the frogs. Suddenly they felt that there was a chance that everything would work out. It's too bad you missed them; they left only a few minutes ago.'

'Well,' sniffed Phyllis, rubbing the wonderfully cool ointment on to her hands, 'that makes me feel much better. What did you all do this afternoon?'

'We had no luck at all,' said Yop bitterly. 'I waited ages by that stupid tree, and Joe has searched every nook and cranny on the whole island, looking for the mandolin.'

'Not quite every one, since I didn't find it,' said Joe. 'But at least Hilary caught some more fish for us. Let's eat! Hilary, do you think those potatoes are done?'

Hilary nodded. 'Yop, do you have any salt in the pockets of your knapsack?'

Yop did, and although the salt in its paper packets had caked after being wet, it crumbled nicely and made the potatoes taste wonderful. In fact, the whole meal was delicious and superbly satisfying.

Hilary swallowed her last mouthful and wiped her mouth with the back of her hand. 'Man told me if I go down to the edge of the Maiden's Island just before dawn, his sister Jonquil will give me some more food. He says the frogs don't watch too carefully during the night because they know we can't see in the dark.'

'I wonder where they got beans and potatoes, of all things,' mused Yop.

'Maybe they grow naturally here,' suggested Hilary.

'Hmm,' said Yop, sounding totally unconvinced, and wondering what was the natural environment for beans and potatoes. Forget it, he thought; there are more important things to think about. 'Anyone for a quick swim? How about you, Phyllis?'

'I haven't finished eating. The hot food burns my sore hands.'

'Man said the water of the Great Pond is good for your cuts. Hey! It can't be good for a mandolin! Are you sure he took it out of the *water*?'

Phyllis nodded. 'It was dripping slime and mud. I wonder if it will still play?'

'I wouldn't worry about that,' said Joe. 'Made by a fish and played by a frog – it must be all right in the water.'

'You've got a point,' said Yop. Something seemed strange about what Joe had just said, but what? Perhaps Joe already knew that the mandolin would still play . . . but he was sure that this was not the point that was bothering him.

He ran with Phyllis down to the beach. 'Pretend we're just fooling around,' he warned, when they were a way out from the shore. 'Keep diving under and swimming back and forth. Let's do somersaults and headstands. And talk softly. You know how sound carries over water.' He dived under and came up again. 'What happened after Joe and I left?'

'I found the mandolin! The frogs said that was what the bush was carrying, and it was right at the place where the bush went to! But I saw Joe polishing it, and it shone like gold. Do you think maybe *he* wants to steal it too?' Her voice rose to a wail.

'Whoa!' said Yop. 'Calm down! You're not making any sense at all. Swim around for a few seconds, and then try again.' He turned over on his back and paddled away.

'Tell me from the beginning,' he urged, when they met again. He glanced at the camp. Hilary and Joe were burying fish bones and making mint tea in the frying pan, and not looking their way at all.

'After I left the frogs, I came down to the far shore,' said Phyllis. 'There's a place about half-way up the island where you can climb down the rocks, before they become too steep. I went very carefully around the corner of the bottom of the cliffs. At first I didn't see the moving bush anywhere. Then I spotted him away down the island, but with half of his branches gone. I suppose he couldn't move fast enough with all of that stuff on him.

'I started running down the beach as quietly as I could, keeping behind whatever rocks I found. I was afraid that if I went too slowly he would get into the forest before I could see where he had gone.

'I stopped behind a big rock half-way down the island, because he turned a little towards me and started climbing up at the end of the cliffs.'

'That's where I first saw you,' said Yop. 'Those branches on the shore must have been part of his disguise.'

'Yes, and do you know what kind of branches they were? The kind whose leaves are used to polish the mandolin! I remember their shape from this morning. Oh, gosh! This morning seems so far away!'

Phyllis sighed deeply and continued, a quiver in her voice. 'The thief kept climbing, and I took a chance on running across under the cliffs when he was going up some really steep parts. When I got close, and after I saw you, *Joe* suddenly came out from behind the rock where the thief had gone! I didn't know what to think!'

'It showed all over you,' laughed Yop.

'It wasn't funny! Joe was polishing the mandolin with some leaves, and holding it up in the sunshine to see the gold, I suppose. He looked so nice and so happy, and I didn't want to believe he's bad! But there were some branches stuck to his clothes, and at first I wondered if maybe he had fought the thief, but I didn't hear or see any fight!' She looked miserably at Yop. 'I hoped maybe there was a good explanation, and he would tell you.'

'No, he behaved as if nothing had happened. But I find it very hard to believe that he's all bad,' frowned Yop. 'I get annoyed with him sometimes, but really, he's always been nice enough . . .'

'Do you think the frogs made a mistake, and it's not their mandolin?'

'Of course not, because it's polished gold. What else could it be? What did it look like?'

'Oh, sort of guitarish, only rounder. But how could Joe have known that the mandolin was in the mud?' asked Phyllis. 'And if he found it by accident, why didn't he tell us? And how did he know which leaves to polish it with? Only Hilary and I saw them this morning. Do you think maybe he's helping the thief? Oh, why does he have to be bad?' Her voice rose again, and Yop pushed her back down in the water.

Yop started a lazy crawl stroke farther into the pond. He thought, and swam, and thought again. What if Joe *was* in league with the thief – why would the thief send *Joe* to get the mandolin? Finding something buried in the mud, particularly while wearing a cumbersome disguise, would be difficult enough even for the person who put it there. A crazy but fascinating idea came into Yop's mind; and the more he thought about it, the more attractive it became. In the meantime . . .

'Where is the mandolin now?' he asked.

'I hid it in the woods behind the camp,' said Phyllis. 'I wanted to give it to the three frogs, but they were gone. Then I thought of bringing it to the stage to see if Man and Kas were there, but how could I when everyone would see me? And it was horribly heavy, and my hands were bleeding again from carrying it so far.'

'We've got to get it to the frogs right away,' said Yop. 'First thing in the morning. We'll give Hilary time to leave for the food, and then we'll take the mandolin. Don't tell Hilary anything. She'll get too upset about Joe.'

'I know,' said Phyllis tremulously. 'But I don't think I can hide how I feel. Maybe Joe will notice that I'm behaving strangely toward him. I can't even look him in the face! He's always been so nice – how can he be a thief?'

'It's a shame,' said Yop, 'but that's not the problem right now. When we get back to camp, say you're tired and go straight to bed. That way you won't have to look at Joe. Once we've got rid of the mandolin it won't matter how you look at him!'

'But I don't want to feel like this. He was our friend!'

Phyllis swallowed a sob. 'And what if we can't find Man and Kas right away?'

'We won't bring it to *them*. We don't know where to find Man and Kas, but we *do* know where there are plenty of other frogs – at the edge of the Maiden's Island!'

13
The Maidenfrog

'Wake up!'

Hilary groaned and raised herself on one elbow.

'It's time to go for the food,' whispered Joe. 'You told me to get you up.'

'OK,' yawned Hilary. 'Oh, I'm so tired.' She came out of the tent on all fours, feeling half asleep and unco-ordinated. 'Why does it have to be me?'

'I don't know. But if Jonquil wants you and only you, there's not much choice, is there? Maybe she's more ready to trust a female.'

'Where's my comb?' Hilary groped for her knapsack, shivering a little. 'It's chilly this morning. Are you sure it's time? I can't see a thing! How do you wake up so early?'

Joe laughed. 'I can wake up whenever I want to. Forget about your hair. No, I shouldn't say that, because as a matter of fact I'd like to borrow your comb. How about letting me use it first though, because you'll have it on you while you're waiting for Jonquil. It'll be dawn in about half an hour, but you should make it a little ahead of time if we don't have too much trouble going over those rocks in the dark.

Let's go. I'll come part of the way with you. Are you feeling better than last night?'

'OK, I think,' said Hilary, feeling disinclined to talk, and so unsociable she almost wished she hadn't confided in Joe the night before.

In spite of the rocks, Joe set a quick pace along the beach, and Hilary was almost glad when he turned back to let her go the last hundred yards or so alone. Her muscles were still cold, she had stumbled more than once, and Joe, for some reason, was unusually impatient.

Only a few seconds after Joe had disappeared back toward the camp, she heard a soft friendly voice call to her from the water. 'Come and talk to me for a few minutes. Jonquil won't be there for a while yet.'

'Oh,' said Hilary dully, 'Gobi.' She crept carefully toward the water, peering through the semi-darkness. 'Oh dear, why am I in such a miserable mood?'

'I told you it would be hard,' said Gobi. 'You'll feel more cheerful when the sun comes up.'

'What good will that do me? Oh, what's the point of this whole mess, anyway? Why is the mandolin so important to the frogs? You told us they didn't even have *one*, in the spring. Why can't they do without it for a little while, or just forget it, if it causes them so many problems?

'Because they can't go backward,' said Gobi, sounding very weary. 'Hilary, you can read, I suppose?'

'Of course I can read!' She squinted through the dim light, wishing she could see Gobi better.

'You've been going to school for years, no doubt. How would you like it if suddenly you had to return to your primary school, and be taught to read again?'

'That wouldn't make any sense. But –'

'The frogs can't go back to singing without a mandolin, either. Every living being has to progress. You've changed since you came here, haven't you? You've learned, and are still learning. Could you go back home and be the same Hilary you were before?'

Hilary was silent. Gradually, understanding came over her. 'It's really that important, isn't it? Those poor frogs. Yes, you're right, I could never be the same again, and I see how they must feel. It would be torture to have to go backward . . . Even if it hurts, I have to go forward now, and so do they. Thanks, Gobi . . . Gobi, why do you sound so tired?'

'Because I've been up all night working on the new mandolin. Whew! Talking to you was a great refresher, dear Hilary. You're in for an exciting day. I'll see you later.'

With a flip and a splash, Gobi was gone. It was gradually getting lighter, and Hilary hurried to cover the few remaining yards to the end of the island, crouching low as she rounded the last curve. She huddled on the shore a little way from the natural bridge, partly behind a bush, and peered into the greyness. Nothing. No noise, and no sign of a friendly frog, or an unfriendly one for that matter.

Those poor little creatures, thought Hilary sadly. Now I understand what they are going through. Reflectively, she unbraided one side of her hair and pulled the comb out from the waistband of her shorts. About half-way through the second braid she was startled almost out of her skin by a little frog who came from nowhere and tugged vigorously at her sleeve.

Hilary gasped and turned reproachfully. She could just make out Jonquil's shape in the semi-light. 'Oh, you startled me!' she protested.

'Sorry, but we have to be very quiet,' breathed the frog. 'Come on, let's go!'

'Go where? Where's the food?'

'It's on the Maiden's Island, of course. Quickly!' Jonquil grabbed Hilary's arm and pulled. 'Keep down low in the water, and don't make a sound. I've got the sentry on this side of the land bridge out of the way for a little while, but there's still one on the other. Come *on!*'

Hilary stayed stubbornly behind her bush. 'But why do I have to go over there? Can't you just bring the food here? We promised we wouldn't go to the Maiden's Island!'

'That's all very well, but the Maidenfrog wants you,' said Jonquil. Quite unaware of the effect of her statement on Hilary, she muttered, 'Not that I'm happy about what she's doing, but I'm a loyal handmaiden-frog, however silly others may be, and her wishes come first, that's what I say!'

Jonquil turned and hopped to the water's edge, and the astonished Hilary scrambled up and followed her. Talk about a promise breaking itself!

'Why does she want *me?*'

'Because you're just the right size. Now, you'd better take your clothes off and hold them above the water. Keep them dry if you can. You *do* have a bathing suit underneath? . . . The tricky bit will be getting on to the island without being seen. When you hear me talking to the other sentry, get up on the bank as quickly as you can and go down the path at the edge of the bridge.'

Jonquil swam ahead and disappeared into the gloom. Numbed by amazement, Hilary found herself obeying Jonquil's orders without hesitation. She gritted her teeth and slid into the cold water and, bent almost double, waded slowly, horribly slowly, across to the other shore. There she crouched, shivering. 'Come on, Jonquil,' she cried inside as her teeth began to chatter.

After a short while a bell-like voice rang out not far away. Hilary turned to see Jonquil's silhouette behind her, high up on the land bridge. 'I have to get back to the Maiden!' said Jonquil. 'What do you suppose is keeping Duke so long?'

'The silly idiot,' came a croak from the far side of the bridge. 'He can't tear himself away!'

'Well, he'll just have to,' said Jonquil, glancing back briefly as Hilary eased herself up on the bank. 'His attachment to the Maiden is almost a mania. It's beginning to frighten me!'

'He'll get over it,' said the sentry. 'You females are just jealous.'

Jonquil snorted. 'Not me! Do you want to go and get him, or shall I?'

'We mustn't leave our posts. Why aren't you watching properly instead of talking to me? Get back to work!'

'I can see quite well from here, thank you!' retorted Jonquil. 'Come to think of it, so could you.' She jumped down and pinched the other frog playfully on the cheek, while Hilary crept noiselessly up the path. 'You can watch both sides for a while. I'll have Duke back in a jiffy.'

The sentry's green spots flashed with embarrassment, and he grumbled angrily deep in his throat.

'Sentries have to control their spots,' chuckled Jonquil, hopping into the forest. 'That's one hurdle over,' she muttered as she approached Hilary. 'But it will be much harder going the other way!'

It was getting light very quickly now. Jonquil and Hilary hurried silently along the path. After a few minutes Jonquil stopped and listened and Hilary waited beside her, rubbing her arms to keep warm. Jonquil pushed her gently into the forest, hissed 'Hide!', and hastened around the bend ahead.

'Well, you silly Duke, was she as lovely as ever?' Jonquil's boisterous voice rang through the forest after what seemed like an age.

'I'm sorry,' rumbled Duke, almost tearfully. 'I just had to see her for myself. I'm so afraid they'll take her away.'

'And wasn't she safe and well?' A third voice, which rippled with patience like a breath of perfume, preceded the frogs around the corner.

'Of course she was,' laughed Jonquil in vibrant, joyful tones.

They're almost an orchestra in themselves, thought Hilary, backing away into the forest and massaging her shaking limbs as vigorously as she dared. I bet they sound wonderful when they sing. Oh, I'm so cold! Hurry up, hurry up!

'You must stop hovering around her like this,' Jonquil was saying. 'She's very patient, but she's bound to get fed up with you.'

'I can't stay away!' said Duke passionately. 'Whenever I think of those humans I feel afraid for her, and then angry, and I hate them so much . . .'

'Your emotions are dangerous,' sighed Jonquil. 'You'd better control them. You're harming yourself, bothering everyone else, and doing no good at all. If she is meant to stay, she'll stay, but neither you nor anyone else will be able to stop her if she has to go.'

She turned to the other frog, completely ignoring Duke, who was quite literally fuming. Vapours, like a smelly green steam, curled out of his mouth and drifted away in the cool dawn air. 'Make sure he gets back to his post, Treasure,' she said.

'Come,' said Treasure. She seemed to be covered with silver stars which flickered gently as she spoke. 'We'll go and inspect the shore together. That will calm you down.' She took Duke by the arm and Jonquil shepherded them both ahead of her.

Boom boom boom, ripple ripple ripple, ding dang dong, went the voices, gradually fading away. Then, suddenly, Jonquil was beside Hilary again.

The trip along the rest of the path to the centre of the Maiden's Island was a flurry of running, stopping, shivering, hiding, watching and avoiding the relatively few frogs on this part of the island. Once they drew back into the woods to watch a bevy of little female frogs with colourful garlands around their necks, chattering and singing as they made their way to the shore.

'They're going to the stage to practise with Man and Kas,' said Jonquil. 'The Maidenfrog told them that if Gobi is making a new mandolin, now is the time to practise harder than ever! Most of the male frogs are still hostile and suspicious, though. So stubborn – just what you'd expect from a male. They say you made up the story of your meeting with Gobi, but how could you? You didn't even know about Gobi until you came here.'

Hilary felt a painful sort of anger clogging her throat. 'News travels fast here,' she commented coolly, and then added shakily, 'I would never do a thing like that.'

'I know, dear,' said Jonquil, patting her hand.

Finally they reached a clearing. In the middle of it was a crude hut of sticks and rushes.

'This is the Maiden's Bower.' Jonquil hesitated as if she did not want to go farther. 'If she leaves, it will be because she chooses to,' she said, a gruff note in her voice. 'I must remember that.'

'What are you talking about?' whispered Hilary. 'If who goes where? The Maidenfrog?'

'Of course, you don't understand. But you will soon. And when you do, please don't judge the frogs too harshly. We love her so much, you see . . .' Jonquil shed a few quick tears, cleared her throat, and smiled sadly. 'Somehow, everything *will* work out for the best.'

She led Hilary up to the door of the hut and peeped inside.

'Is she here? Bring her in!' An excited human voice was followed by an eager hand, dragging Hilary through the doorway. Shocked, Hilary found herself being hugged and squeezed, by a young woman of much her own size. 'Oh, thank you for coming! Are those your clothes? Let me borrow them!'

Hilary dropped the clothes helplessly into the girl's hand. 'Wh-what? Who-'

'You weren't expecting me, were you?' giggled the girl, throwing off a white dress and pulling on Hilary's shorts and top over her own bathing suit. 'A red shirt! Wonderful! That suits my mood perfectly, just now. My name is Chrys, short for Chrysanthemum, and you're Hilary, right? Welcome to my Bower.' She looked mischievously at Hilary's astonished face. 'My frogs keep their secrets well, don't they? If only they weren't so afraid! Hmm . . . I'll have to have braids, like you. That's the closest we'll get to my hair looking like yours. Oh, you have a comb. Good. Mine has lost most of its teeth.'

Chrysanthemum's hair was long and curly, a lighter brown than Hilary's, with golden streaks from the sun. She had a pretty, cheerful face, sparkling eyes, and a sharp, decisive way of moving. She forced the comb through her hair and braided it rapidly, while she continued to chatter to Hilary and Jonquil.

'Look at her, poor thing, she's freezing! Dry her off, Jonquil, and give her my dress. Warm yourself over the fire, Hilary, and make yourself some herb tea. Jonquil will show you everything. There's no time to explain, but please, please stay here out of sight until I get back. I have to talk to the man who has the mandolin, but the frogs absolutely mustn't know. If they see me leaving the island, I hope they'll think I'm you, stealing food. Now where's that bag of vegetables?'

'I hope you can find him,' said Hilary. 'We haven't even seen him!'

'Oh, come now, I saw one of you with him just yesterday! They seemed perfectly friendly, too!'

Hilary looked horrified. 'That's impossible!'

'Oh, no, I'd know him anywhere. He's cut his hair a little, and changed clothes since the first time I saw him, but it was him, I'm sure.' Her eyes twinkled. 'And if he has any sense, he'll be on the lookout for me. He has to give me back the mandolin, and we've got to talk, and it's impossible for him to come here!'

Chrys peeped out the door, and then smiled back at

104

them. 'All clear. Take care of her, Jonquil. Thank you! Goodbye!'

14
Escape with the Mandolin

When the whispering had died away Phyllis came out of the tent and crept over to the sleeping Yop. She had awakened because it was suddenly cooler in the tent without Hilary snuggling up beside her. It was strange to feel thankful to wake up cold.

'Yop! Yop! We have to get the mandolin *now*!'

Yop rolled over and opened his eyes. 'Huh?'

'Joe and Hilary have just left to get the food. He's going with her part of the way. We've only got a few minutes. Come on, come on, we may not get another chance.'

'You're right,' said Yop, waking fully and standing up. 'He'll expect us to build up the fire and sit around waiting for breakfast.'

Phyllis shuddered. 'I just thought of something else. What if the real thief knows it's missing, and is waiting to catch us?'

'I don't think there's much chance of that,' said Yop. 'Let's go.'

'What do you mean?' asked Phyllis. 'How do you know?'

Yop groaned impatiently. 'I lay awake a long time

last night thinking about everything you told me, and I doubt if we have to worry about anyone except Joe Harris coming after us, but there's no time to explain it now. I'm not sure about it anyway, so we'll be extra careful, just in case.'

They left the camp in a great hurry, Phyllis still demanding explanations, and then spent several minutes blundering around in the dark woods trying to find the mandolin.

'I could see it easily if it was light,' wailed Phyllis. 'It was near two trees, and – Oh! My hands can't take any more of these brambles!'

'Could you see the camp from where you hid it?' asked Yop. 'Try to judge how far away you were, and where the fire was in relation to you. I'll go down and stir up the embers so you can see them.'

Phyllis was almost in despair, after rushing from one pair of trees to another and finding the location of the fire no use at all, when she suddenly realized why. 'Oh, I remember! There were two more trees in front of them, and so I couldn't see the fire at all from where I hid it. I wanted to be sure no-one could see me.'

'Come on, come on!' said Yop. 'He'll be back any minute!'

'I found it!' cried Phyllis triumphantly.

'Shhh! Give it to me,' said Yop. 'It's not that heavy! Maybe it was just waterlogged last night.'

He hustled Phyllis up the end of the island. They would not be able to cut through the woods, particularly in the dark, without making too much noise; and keeping in the open would probably be faster anyway.

It was quite a bit lighter by the time they had covered most of the distance along the top of the cliffs on the far side of the island. Yop stopped to have a long look at the mandolin.

Slowly a delighted smile spread over his face. 'I wish I had one of those leaves to polish it with, just to be sure.'

'Here,' said Phyllis. She dug in the pocket of her shorts. 'I kept a few yesterday. Maybe it's too wilted to use. Be quick, we have to keep going!'

The leaf was of the thick, rubbery sort that wilts reluctantly. 'It would have to be tough,' said Yop, rubbing hard, 'to stand all this friction.'

Before long the mandolin began to glow gently with its own golden light. 'Wow, it's lovely,' marvelled Yop. 'I wish we had this kind of wood in our world. Imagine what beautiful things you could carve in it! But, look, don't you recognize it?'

'Recognize what? The wood?'

'The mandolin. Doesn't it look very like Joe's guitar?'

Phyllis stared. 'Yes. No, it can't be! What are you saying? Anyway, it's not the same colour. His was lighter.'

'It's still quite wet,' said Yop. 'What do you want to bet that when it's dry it looks *exactly* like his?'

Phyllis opened her mouth to protest, and then froze, as a jay flew up from the woods below with a startled shriek. 'Something scared that bird! Maybe he's coming! . . .'

'I think I hear someone . . . It was stupid of me to stop and polish the mandolin,' said Yop, 'but it was such a temptation!' He motioned to Phyllis and they moved forward slowly, keeping to the edge of the woods. 'Down!' he hissed suddenly, and they huddled just behind some bushes, waiting.

They could hear the sounds distinctly now, coming closer, the sharp crackle of twigs snapping as someone came up through the woods. There's no time to go forward, thought Yop. We're too close to where he's sure to come out if he's going to get the mandolin. Breathlessly they watched, while Joe passed not twenty yards in front of them and began climbing quickly down the rocks.

'We're really in a jam,' whispered Yop. 'We don't dare come out while he can see us, and once he's found that the mandolin isn't there, he'll be *looking* for us. We'll have to run for it!'

'Let's worm along the ground until he's gone far enough down,' said Phyllis. She lay flat and inched toward the edge of the cliffs.

'It's not easy with this mandolin,' grunted Yop.

A few minutes went by, and Phyllis said, 'I can't see him any more.'

'OK. Keep close to the trees and as low as you can, and remember that we're going straight for the Maiden's Island.'

'What if he sees us, and follows us there?'

'I don't know. I hadn't thought of that. I just don't know . . .' After a long pause, Yop shrugged and said cheerfully, 'I just hope he doesn't! Now, let's go!'

It was a wild and exciting run, bent over, heads turning again and again back toward the rocks. Yop was ready to burst with exultation as they approached the meadow leading to the peach trees. Just a little farther and they would be out of sight! Then they heard a shout from behind.

'Yop! Wait!'

There was Joe up on the skyline, a dreadful, threatening figure in Phyllis's overwrought mind. She gave a little cry and ran on. Yop followed her furiously.

'Humans, humans!' The frog sentries croaked and jumped about in terror as Yop and Phyllis came pounding down the slope toward them. 'Stop, stop!'

A horde of frogs materialized from the woods on the Maiden's Island, shrieking and crying, and frightening Phyllis so much that it took all her courage to carry on. Yop waved the mandolin in front of him. 'Look!' he heaved desperately, 'we've got the mandolin, but he's chasing us –'

'We have to find a safe place to put it!' squealed Phyllis, putting her arms over her face to shield herself from the deluge of frogs. 'Please! –'

As quickly as they had appeared from nowhere, the frogs leapt around Phyllis and Yop and their beloved mandolin, and closed like a chattering, flickering wave behind them, driving them on to the Maiden's Island.

Dimly, as he plunged into the trees, Yop heard a seagull calling. It was not until much later that it occured to him that he had never seen a gull on this inland lake.

15

A Great Commotion

Left alone in the Maiden's Bower, Hilary and Jonquil looked uneasily at each other for a few seconds. Jonquil was a pretty frog with white and yellow spots, and a good-natured face clouded at the moment by worry.

Jonquil pressed her hands to her big cheeks and tinkled, 'Oh, I hope I've done right, but I'm so afraid she'll have to leave us... The others will never forgive me if she goes. They'll say it's all my fault! But can't they see that it has to be left up to her?' She gulped on a sob. 'Oh, stop this nonsense, Jonquil; you have work to do! Look at this poor child here, still shivering and shaking!'

She took Hilary's wet bathing suit, helped her into the white dress and handed her a tattered grey blanket. 'See, the water is almost boiling. Tea will warm you up. Here are the mint leaves. You'll have to make it yourself; I'm not strong enough to lift the pan. Oh dear, oh dear, what use will the mandolin be without her?'

Hilary made the tea and sipped a little. She was feeling warmer and calmer now, and more and more curious. Who was that nice girl? It seemed, unbelievably, that she was the Maidenfrog; but who was she really, and where did she come from? Hilary liked her. That's someone, she thought, that I'd like to have for a friend.

And what a pleasant little cottage this was! Had Chrysanthemum built it herself, or had the frogs done it? There was a little fireplace in one side, with a stone chimney, and the pan Jonquil had mentioned boiling over the fire. There were beans and some root vegetables, and a few wooden pots. Almost everything was very rustic and primitive-looking, except for a few items, like the pan, a few books and Chrysanthemum's clothes, which must have been made somewhere else.

Jonquil rambled on and on, interspersing her lamentations with offers of food and drink. 'How about some potato cake with honey? The Maiden loves it, and you will too.'

'What do you call her, the Maiden or the Maidenfrog?' ventured Hilary.

'Really, she should be called the Frog Maiden,' said Jonquil, 'because she's a maiden living with the frogs. But the frogs wanted to make her sound as if she really was one of them, instead of a human being, so they named her the Maidenfrog. The Maiden is short for either of them. It's the same with the name of this island – Maidenfrog's Island or Frog Maiden's Island are just too long and awkward.

'Have another potato cake.' Jonquil's coloured spots began to pulse strongly. She was about to say something that was very close to her heart. 'Please try to understand. She was lost, and we found her. We were afraid, but we nursed her and cared for her when she was ill and covered with insect bites. And now, somehow, she *belongs* to us . . . But we mustn't encourage ourselves to believe that she'll stay for ever. And Duke is making it worse for everyone. He has become so terribly attached to her, so full of anger and fear, that he can't even harmonize properly any more, but he stubbornly refuses to admit it. I try to explain to him that humans are her natural family, and that he should want what's best for her, but he won't listen. Why would she ever want to stay here, when she can be with her own kind?' Jonquil sobbed, sniffed and bowed her head miserably.

Hilary stirred honey into her second cup of tea. The clink of her spoon against the cup was the only sound in the uncomfortable silence. What could she possibly say to comfort this wonderful, selfless little frog?

'I – I'm sure she loves you all very much,' said Hilary, and then the uproar began.

Jonquil jumped and fluttered to the door. 'Whatever can that be?'

'They must have seen her leaving!' exclaimed Hilary.

'Maybe I can persuade them it was only you! Oh dear, oh dear,' said Jonquil distractedly, 'such troubles! You stay here in the bower and drink your tea. If you hear anyone coming, lie down on the bed and cover yourself as much as possible with the blanket. No one would dare to disturb the Maiden when she's sleeping . . .'

Jonquil hopped in an agitated way out of the door, leaving Hilary alone with her tea and her thoughts.

'Not that way! Take the left fork!' shrieked several frogs, effectively turning Yop and Phyllis off the path to the Maiden's Bower. They blundered deeper and deeper into a dark and gloomy part of the forest, until there was almost no path at all.

Phyllis stopped and leaned against a tree. 'I just can't go any farther,' she wailed, out of breath. The wave of frogs parted around her and continued after Yop, except for one little frog who squatted beside her.

'He's not following us any more,' squeaked the frog.

'He's not?' gasped Phyllis.

'He didn't even cross over to the Maiden's Island,' continued the frog. 'I saw him. He went to meet one of your people on the other island. She made a strange cry when she was running up the meadow, and when he noticed her, he stopped chasing you and followed her instead.'

'Oh, no!' said Phyllis. 'He's going to take Hilary hostage!'

Hilary finished her tea and potato cake, and put her bathing suit, which had dried rapidly over the fire, on under the dress. The sounds of the commotion were less now, and suddenly she felt incredibly tired. The bed looked so inviting! Just to be on the safe side, she thought, I'll lie down and cover myself up . . .

Within a few minutes Hilary was deeply asleep.

Yop and the crowd of frogs finally stopped when they reached the shore of the Great Pond on the far side of the Maiden's Island.

'Where do we go now?' asked Yop.

'Give it to us! Give it to us!' chirped the frogs. 'We'll hide it.'

Yop handed over the mandolin, and several little frogs, followed by the rest, dragged it off along the shore. He watched them, frowning, a half-idea drifting into his head.

'Let me escort you off the island,' said a dry voice beside him. Who should it be, but Andu!

Yop looked down at Andu, and at Uka, who was beside him.

'You've got a nerve!' he said. 'I bring you your precious mandolin, and you still want to get rid of me! I thought maybe this would prove to you that I'm not so bad after all.'

'So you did it just to get in with us?' said Uka mournfully. 'Tch, tch!'

'Typical, calculating human behaviour,' added Andu.

Yop reddened, sputtering, 'I brought it back because it was yours!'

Andu looked unblinkingly back at Yop. 'I never know what to believe with you humans.'

'That's because you don't want to believe anything good.'

Andu shrugged. 'In any case, we thank you for what you did, regardless of your motives. But now that we have the mandolin back, we can't risk having you here. You must find your friends and go home.'

'It's not fair,' said Yop disgustedly. 'What if I go and see the island for myself?'

Andu gaped at him. 'You wouldn't! –'

'No, I wouldn't,' muttered Yop. 'But it makes me angry that you won't believe me. What have I done to deserve this kind of treatment?'

Andu was silent. He looked at Uka, and Uka looked back at him. 'Nothing,' croaked Andu eventually. 'You're a little obnoxious, but really, you have done nothing wrong.'

'Well, then –?'

'Yop! Yop!' Phyllis came stumbling through the trees. 'He's got Hilary! He's keeping her as a hostage!'

Phyllis's explanation came tumbling out. Yop stared at her in horror, all thoughts of the Maiden's Island effectively ousted from his mind.

'He was right,' said Uka, as the cousins hurried away.

'I know,' glowered Andu. 'Why does he have to be right? There's too much at stake to risk trusting him . . . Oh, will we ever be rid of these humans? – Rid of all humans but one!'

16
An Explosion

High up on the cliffs, the thief and the Maidenfrog
walked and talked, oblivious of everything but each
other.

'I'm sorry I couldn't give the mandolin back to you
myself,' said the thief.

'It doesn't matter,' said Chrys. 'I'm just so happy to
be here. But what a silly situation! There I was on my
island, dying to come across and talk to you, never
dreaming that the frogs would be so stubborn. They
told me they would get the mandolin back themselves,
because you (being a thief) weren't a proper person for
me to meet. As if I couldn't see through that! I suppose
you didn't get much time to play the mandolin, with
the frogs following you all over the place!'

'At first, no. They were terribly persistent! Afterwards, though,' grinned the thief, 'I had plenty of time
to practise!'

'What can you possibly mean?'

The thief explained.

'How fanastic!' said Chrys, laughing, when he had
finished. 'That girl Hilary is nice. Poor thing, I really
took her by surprise. And the three of them come from

another world! I'd love to visit it some day. Well! Those cunning frogs of mine knew all the time that there was another world through the whirlpool, and they never told me! I wondered how three children could possibly have arrived here just like that!' Suddenly she turned solemn. 'But what are we going to do now? Do you know your way back through the swamp to civilization?'

'I made a map – if only the frogs haven't ransacked my boat.'

'Oh, no, I took care of that. I told them to hide the boat but not to disturb your belongings, so you'd be able to leave as soon as you gave up the mandolin. It's going to be very hard to tell them that I'll have to go, too. They don't want me to leave; in fact they're desperate about keeping me here, but they don't understand. I can't stay here for the winter. I'll starve, or die of the cold!'

'We'll come back in the spring,' said the thief.

'Yes,' said Chrys, 'but even that will be easier said than done. However will we explain this place to our families and friends?'

The thief chuckled at the thought, and hugged Chrysanthemum. 'We'll manage it somehow,' he said, shrugging.

'Oh!' said Chrys, a few seconds later. 'I don't even know your name!'

'My name is Joheres,' said the thief.

Hilary woke and opened her eyes. She had rolled over on her back, as she always did when she slept, and lay luxuriously gazing at the chinks of blue sky through the roof of the bower. For a few moments she felt wonderfully relaxed and happy, and then a wave of anxiety and fear washed over her. She turned her head toward the door.

'Aaah! Aaah! Oooooh!'

Duke the frog, who had been staring at Hilary, screamed, a long, shrill, desperate, agonized scream, and blundered from the hut.

'The Maidenfrog,' he gasped, 'the Maidenfrog ... she's gone!' He gulped in huge breaths of air. His bubble and then his whole body began to swell.

Hilary jumped up and ran over to the door. Duke was only a few yards outside the bower, expanding rapidly. Hilary stared in terror as the frog grew bigger and bigger and bigger.

Boom!

Green liquid spewed everywhere, horrible, stinking liquid, over Hilary, over the lovely bower and the whole sunlit clearing. Then the empty shell of Duke, crumpled like a burst balloon, lay still on the ground.

Hilary ran desperately down the path, calling, 'Help! Help! He's exploded!'

Half-way to the land bridge, where the path divided, she surprised Jonquil and Treasure coming from the direction followed by Phyllis and Yop and the horde of frogs.

'Whatever is the matter?'

'You shouldn't be here!' scolded Jonquil. 'You must stay hidden until the Maiden returns. Your friends have brought back the mandolin, so everything may work out all right, if only she comes soon! Hurry, hurry!'

'Just a minute, Jonquil,' said Treasure. 'Let her speak. What's that smell?' she added sharply. 'It reeks of anger, and hatred –'

'It's Duke!' cried Hilary. 'He's exploded! He saw me in the bower, and he blew up!'

'Oh, dear me!' fluttered Treasure, and hopped off toward the clearing.

Jonquil pressed her hands to her head and thought for a minute. 'Go and get Chrysanthemum. And the healing balm. Do you still have it?'

'It's at the camp,' nodded Hilary.

'Hurry, then. It's our only chance. We can try to mend him, and if the Maidenfrog is with him, maybe he'll want to live. Run! And wash yourself, for heaven's sake – get rid of that disgusting smell. Oh, what a job we have before us!'

A half-developed thought still nagged at the back of Yop's mind as he and Phyllis returned to the thief's island. To add to this minor irritation, Yop had no idea what he and Phyllis were going to do now. And they were both getting hungry.

They hurried over to the peach trees, and it was from there, while they munched gratefully on the juicy fruit, that they saw Joe and his hostage high up on the cliffs. They seemed to be picking and eating blackberries. Joe was carrying a bag, no doubt full of the food Hilary had gone to get. Hilary didn't look like a prisoner, but suddenly Joe grabbed her by the hand and they disappeared down into the woods.

Where could they be going? Back to the camp, most likely. 'We'll go there, too,' said Yop. 'I can't see what harm he could possibly do to all three of us. And it's not fair if they get all the food.'

They went quickly up through the trees and across the island. 'I still wish I knew what he wants the mandolin for,' said Yop, when they were within a few minutes of reaching the camp. 'Surely he wouldn't upset all these frogs, just to play a silly mandolin! –'

A blinding flash of enlightenment hit Yop. He stopped and pounded his fists against a tree, laughing as softly as he could, wanting to shout and crow. 'That's it! The mandolin isn't played by a frog! It's played by a human!'

He grabbed Phyllis by the shoulders and shook her eagerly. 'Didn't you see how heavy it was for them? No, you weren't there. Well, it took six of them to drag it off into the woods. Haven't you seen their fingers? They aren't long enough to play the mandolin – in fact some of the frogs' fingers are webbed!'

'Stop shaking me, you idiot!' said Phyllis. 'I believe you. But so what?'

'They've got a human being here, stupid. That's why they talked about the purest of the pure dwelling here, thanks to the swamps and so on. It's a pure *human*! That's why they weren't worried about offending me with their stupid little rhymes. It's someone *else* they don't want to offend!'

'But why would they want to hide a human from us?' asked Phyllis.

'There must be some good reason,' said Yop, continuing on toward the camp. 'Let me think.'

'And that reminds me, why won't you tell me what you worked out about Joe, last night?'

'You're going to know in a minute anyway,' said Yop. 'There's Joe. Do you see him? He's eating. It's not fair. I'm starving.'

'Wait a minute,' said Phyllis, holding his arm. 'That's not Hilary with him!'

'You're right, it's not! What did I tell you? Looking

friendly, aren't they? Well! Let's go talk to the Maiden-frog and the thief!'

'Hey! Help!' Hilary's breathless cry came from down the beach just as Yop and Phyllis burst out of the woods.

Joheres and Chrys stood up in astonishment at this two-sided invasion of their privacy.

'Hilary! What is it? Look! I found him, just as I said I would!' Chrys held Joheres happily by the arm. 'He was running down the end of this island, and I got his attention with a seagull call! I knew he'd notice – we're much too far from the sea for gulls. And by the way – he didn't really steal the mandolin. I lent it to him.'

Hilary staggered to a halt and hesitated, looking wide-eyed at Chrys and Joe. 'But, what – ? Oh, there's no time for that now. It's Duke! He exploded! Please go and help him, Chrys. And take the healing balm.'

She reached down into her knapsack and turned to give the little wooden pot to the Maidenfrog, but Chrys was already racing down the beach. She put it into the hand of the waiting Joheres. 'Jonquil says it's the only chance!'

Hilary sank wearily down on the sand and looked up at the concerned faces of her sister and cousin. 'I'm all right,' she said. 'Just a little too much for one day, and it's not over yet.'

'You smell terrible,' said Phyllis frankly.

'I know,' said Hilary. 'I'll wash. But first we'd better go and find Man. He's at the stage, practising. He has to be told what has happened.'

17
Clean-up

'How can we tell him?' asked Phyllis. They were close to the stage now, and the sweetness of the frog music washed like a cry of pain through her heart. 'What if – what if Man explodes too?'

'What choice is there?' shrugged Yop. He put the last piece of cold left-over potato in his mouth and wiped his hands. 'All we can do is tell them, and then wait for the panic to die down.'

'Oh, I wish we didn't have to!'

'Wishing won't do any good,' said Hilary bluntly, feeling very cold and hard inside. 'It's my news, and I can handle it . . . Man! Man!' she shouted loudly above the choir, and then louder still to arouse the frogs from their absorption. Man turned, looking startled, and so did Kas and the handful of frogs, mostly female, that they were directing. Phyllis recognized her three little friends, but felt only sorrow at having to see them again now.

'Man! You are needed on the Maiden's Island. Duke has exploded!'

'Aaiiee!' Man's hands flew to his head as if to shut

out the terrible news. 'Aaiiee!' he wailed, 'what further misery am I to be responsible for?'

'Stop it, Man!' said Kas. 'Duke did this to himself. It's not your fault!'

But Man continued to wail and wail. His cries were so loud and penetrating that they drove Hilary, Yop and Phyllis cringing back to the shore.

'What a drag this is,' said Yop, troubled in spite of himself. 'What do we do now?'

'Go and help the frogs, of course!' said Phyllis and Hilary together.

'But I'll have to wash first,' added Hilary. 'You two get started.' She watched them hurry along the shore, and waded into the pond to clean up. Before long she had successfully removed the stink, if not the ugly green stain, from the white dress. She wrung it out and spread it over a branch, and then lay back in the sun, letting its rays penetrate and warm her whole body, which still seemed to be shivering to the core. I wish I could go fishing, she said to herself, and just get away from it all.

Those poor frogs, she kept thinking over and over, those poor frogs. So much suffering, so much misery, and why? Surely this isn't the right way for the frogs to do – to do what they were created for! She remembered suddenly what Joe had said the night before . . . something about the incredible purposefulness of the frogs. Certainly they were confused, certainly they were doing some things the wrong way – but over and above all this, they one and all were consumed with the supreme purpose of singing – of doing what they were created for.

Hilary got up slowly, her mind clinging to this one last thought. I've got it! she said to herself. I do believe

I've got it! She gathered up her fishing tackle and, feeling like crying and singing at the same time, almost flew down the beach.

Gobi was working on the mandolin, waiting for Hilary. 'Well?' he asked.

'It's my purpose that I'm looking for, Gobi!' she cried. 'I have to find out what I was created for. Isn't that it?'

'You don't have to ask me,' answered Gobi, 'if you *know*, that's right!' He paused in his work and looked with immense satisfaction at Hilary and then at the mandolin. 'See, the mandolin is almost finished. Isn't it lovely? A beautiful job! It will be waiting for Joheres when you come back. He is eagerly waiting for his own mandolin.'

'I don't understand it all,' said Hilary. 'Yop ran off saying something about Joe Harris being the thief, and belonging to this world, but I don't see how it's possible . . .'

'Your cousin will explain everything. He's very sharp, that boy.'

It seemed unnecessary to ask Gobi how he knew anything at all about Yop, whom he had never met.

'To tell the truth, I feel rather embarrassed about Joe,' confided Hilary, staring down at her hands.

'You're just looking at things the wrong way,' said Gobi. 'Remember – all angles of the problem at once!' He laughed and wiggled his eyes. 'You had an interesting experience knowing him; you learned something about yourself; and now you should be happy for both Chrys and Joe (and for the frogs, incidentally, who have to be forced to take what's good for them).' He paused. 'You weren't seriously thinking of marrying him, were you?'

Hilary sat up, looking stunned. 'Oh! No! Good heavens, no! I'm much too young!'

'Well, there you are,' said Gobi. 'Maybe she isn't.' He paused to let that sink in.

'I *am* happy for them,' Hilary said suddenly, a note of discovery in her voice. 'Of course I am!'

'You won't be staying here much longer,' continued Gobi. 'Put Phyllis's pretty stones in your knapsack, so that she won't forget them, and give Yop this piece of goldwood. He can carve what he likes with it, but unfortunately it won't shine in your world. I'll leave it by the new mandolin; you can pick them up together.'

'OK.' Hilary hesitated, looking expectant.

'You've already been given what the Great Pond had for you, Hilary,' said Gobi, grinning.

'I suppose so,' sighed Hilary, feeling a little disappointed just the same. 'But Gobi, my mind is still so full of questions . . . This may seem silly, but are you sure I have a purpose? It's such a strange idea, being created for a special reason! It can't have to do with whether I'll be a doctor, or a dancer, or whatever, because one person can do many things. It has to be something greater, something –' She spread her hands in yearning. 'Maybe I shouldn't ask you, Gobi, but do you know what I was created for?'

'You were right in thinking perhaps you shouldn't ask me that,' chuckled Gobi, 'but only because I don't know the answer. You'll have to find that in your own world. How fortunate you are! Starting on a treasure hunt, with a certain reward at the end of it!'

'But how will I find it? These frogs at least are told what their purpose is, but I –'

'If my experience of life and creation is anything to judge by, you humans are doubtless told, too. Real treasures are clear and visible to those whose eyes are really looking. Search, my dear,' said Gobi. 'Search, ask for guidance, be sincere, and you will find the answer. That I can promise you.'

After a long silence, Hilary asked, 'Will poor Duke be all right?'

'What do you think?'

'If he looks at it from the right angle . . .'

'. . . then he'll be just fine. Obviously. But whether or not he can do that depends on many things. He's going to need help.'

'Treasure will help him, I think,' said Hilary. 'She's well-named.'

Gobi leapt into the water. 'Go and fish now, Hilary – from the Maiden's Island, if you like – and when you have caught enough for supper, join the others. That's the best help you can give them right now; they'll all be ravenous by the end of the afternoon.' He blew her a round, bubbly kiss that burst when it reached her lips. 'Off with you, Hilary! Go be wise!'

Phyllis and Yop stood near the land bridge and watched the shore of the Maiden's Island. There was no sign of anyone to prevent them from crossing over.

'Why shouldn't we go?' said Yop. 'We know all their secrets now.'

'I just think maybe they've had enough of humans,' said Phyllis.

'What a horrible smell!' said Yop. 'It's like all the bad smells you can think of mixed up together. It makes me feel quite sick. What must it be like where he exploded?'

Two little frogs came hopping out of the woods, down

to the water's edge, and filled tiny wooden pots with water. They seemed not to notice Phyllis and Yop. After a minute or so another two appeared on the same errand. This time one frog stopped and stared at the humans with big, sad eyes, shed a few tears, turned away and went back into the forest with his companion.

'Gosh, they really know how to make you feel bad,' said Yop.

'There must be *something* we can do to help,' said Phyllis. 'I'm going over.'

Two more frogs came out of the trees and leapt forward to meet Phyllis. They were her friends from the day before.

'Oh, dear Phyllis Human,' cried one, tears pouring down its face.

'He won't make it,' sniffed the other. 'We can't fill him up.'

'Fill him up? With what?'

'With water. If he's dry too long, he'll die!'

'Your gardener is helping. He's carrying pots full, but it's running out of the holes. The Maidenfrog can't sew him up fast enough.'

'I knew we could help!' said Phyllis joyfully. 'Yop can carry water, and I'll sew.'

It was a long and exhausting afternoon. Phyllis crouched with Chrysanthemum on the foul-smelling ground by the bower, stitching up the motionless Duke with a thick rough thread made of reeds. The threads were quite short – only as long as the reeds they came from – so there was an endless process of threading the fishbone needle, stitching, tying a knot and starting all over again. Little frogs jumped in and around their arms under the direction of Jonquil and Treasure, lubricating the seams with healing balm and stuffing small holes with moss.

Yop and Joe went back and forth to the shore with the saucepan and two metal cups from the hut. Once they waited on the shore for a few seconds, watching some frogs build a raft of sticks and reeds, while they regained their courage to return to the clearing. It seemed that every time they came back toward the bower, they had to adjust to the incredible stench all over again. 'How do the girls bear it?' asked Yop wearily.

'We'd better let them carry water for a while,' said Joe. First Joe took Chrys's place, but she would not stay away from Duke for more than one trip at a time. Then Yop replaced Phyllis. 'I don't think I can stay here for long, Phyllis,' he said grittily. 'The smell makes me feel so sick!'

'I don't quite understand all that's happened,' said Phyllis to Joe on the way to the pond, 'but I'm so glad you're still our friend. I was so upset to think you were a thief!'

'I'll explain it all tonight,' said Joe, hugging her. 'It would have been a lot simpler if I had been straight with you all from the start, but like the frogs, I really didn't know what was the right thing to do!'

When they got back to the clearing, Yop grabbed the two metal cups as soon as Phyllis had emptied them and ran off into the forest, where he was horribly sick. 'Sorry,' he said to Phyllis when she followed him almost immediately with the pot. 'I just couldn't stand it.'

'That's OK,' said Phyllis. 'You don't have to be Superman. Joe and I will take turns sewing.'

The job was not made easier by many of the frogs,

who looked at their human helpers with bitter, accusing stares. At one point, Andu passed Yop on his way from the shore, and said to Uka, quite loudly, 'I suppose they'll make a picnic area next, and all bring their dogs!'

'Dogs, yes!' said Uka. 'Don't you just love their sharp teeth and playful ways?'

Finally a few inches of water would stay in the bottom of Duke's patched-up body.

'That's enough for now,' said Jonquil. 'Let's move him on to the raft. Would you humans carry him to the pond? There we can irrigate him all the time.' She looked almost happy. 'This is the first time we've been able to save a grown frog that exploded. Sometimes a very young frog barely past the tadpole stage misjudges its capacity or has a tantrum and explodes, but they are so little and mend so quickly that we can just put them back in the pond with a few stitches until they heal.'

'But it's not yet certain that he'll survive. And he will never sing again.' It was the first thing Man had said during the whole afternoon. He looked almost as deflated as Duke.

'If only I had discouraged him from becoming so attached to me,' said Chrys sadly, 'perhaps this would never have happened . . . Why does it smell so bad? Ordinary frog spit isn't nice, but it's never like this!'

'It's the smell of hatred,' said Treasure, 'and anger and fear . . . How can it help but be horrible?'

'Much of this mess could have been avoided if everyone had been straightforward and truthful and fearless right from the start,' said Jonquil briskly. 'But it's too late to change that. Pick him up very carefully, and let's get moving. We – all of us – can only do our best.'

Poor Duke became conscious for a second as Yop and Joe raised him from the ground. His eyes grew huge and anguished, perhaps due to the pain of his wounds, or perhaps because he saw who was carrying him. Then he fainted clean away.

18
Chrysanthemum's Story

'Hello,' said Hilary. 'I'm going to see if Chrys has some more vegetables for us. How has it been? What are you carrying? Oh, it's Duke!' She winced and hurried by, avoiding the frogs who were following Yop and Joe. 'He'll be all right,' she muttered to herself.

'Why do you say that?' asked Treasure, at the tail end of the procession.

'Oh!' said Hilary, going red, and then pale once more. 'Gobi said that if only Duke looks at it from the right angle . . .'

'Duke has never been much good at that,' said Treasure.

'Maybe you can help him,' answered Hilary shyly. 'You seem to be all patience.'

Chrysanthemum stood in the middle of the clearing looking forlornly at her ruined home, while Phyllis gathered up its contents in a few rush bags.

'I'll never be able to stay here again. My lovely bower!'

'You can have our tent,' said Hilary. 'We'll get another one back in our world. And you can keep my comb and my clothes, too. Your white dress looks just awful now.'

'Thank you,' said Chrys, smiling. 'I wish you didn't have to leave. We could be such good friends.'

'I know,' said Hilary. 'But we'll still be friends, even if we don't see each other. And maybe someday we'll come back, or you'll visit our world. Look! I've caught supper. Have you got any more vegetables? We can all eat together at our camp.'

Chrys brought Hilary to a little garden behind the bower. Fortunately, the hut had largely protected it from the explosion.

'You planted it?' asked Hilary.

'Yes, there were a few potatoes and beans stowed in my boat. The potatoes I gave you yesterday were the first ones I've dug up. Usually, I eat these other potatoes. They grow wild here. That's what the potato cakes were made of.'

'They look like Jerusalem artichokes,' said Hilary. 'My mother makes pickles with them.' It was strange but very comforting to be able to talk of such mundane subjects as gardening and cooking, in the midst of all the chaos and misery.

They brought the vegetables into the bower, and put them in the remaining rush bag.

'How did you get here in the middle of nowhere, all by yourself?' asked Phyllis.

'I was on a field trip in the spring with some other students,' said Chrys. 'We went into the swamp in groups each day, collecting samples of plants, insects and so on. It was terrific fun. We had to be very careful to make maps of where we went, though, because it's easy to get lost in the swamp, and it's dotted with lakes that all look alike.

'One day when I had taken a boat out by myself on one of the lakes, to catch fish for everyone's supper, a storm came up. It happened so quickly that I had barely enough time to take apart my fishing rod and duck down in the bottom of the boat. When at last the wind died down and the lake became calm again, I tried to find my way home.

'But the red marker I had tied to a tree to show where I had come out of the swamp had blown away! I rowed around looking for somewhere familiar, but everything looked the same. I couldn't even try to guide myself by the sun, because the sky was still overcast.

'I called for help, but there was no answer. I expect everyone was just too far away. I rowed a little way into the swamp, where it was more sheltered, because it was quickly getting dark. The best plan seemed to be to stay still until morning when, I hoped, people would come to look for me.

'It was a miserable night. I was wet and cold, and my mosquito repellant had been washed off by the rain, so the mosquitoes were all over me. I ate the few biscuits that I had left, lay down in the bottom of the boat, and eventually fell asleep.

'I dreamt of beautiful singing voices. When I woke up, I seemed to still hear them for a while, and then they faded away. I rowed in the direction from which the voices had come and called out, but got no answer. Then I went through the whole process again – sleeping, dreaming, waking full of hope, and rowing desperately. This time I came out of the swamp on to a lake. After a third dream I rowed a long, long way, and found myself, at dawn, near these islands. I reached the shore and collapsed. Later I realized that the voices I had been following were those of the frogs, but how I could hear them from so far away, I'll never understand.

'The frogs took me in and cared for me. They fed me, and kept me warm and sheltered in this little hut which had been built by humans who had been here before.' She stopped, sighed, and went inside the bower to take a last look. 'Maybe by next spring the rains will have washed away the smell.

'Anyway, those wonderful frogs put healing balm and water from the Great Pond on my bites and bruises, and there were no mosquitoes to bother me because the frogs ate them! I was very ill – I wonder if perhaps I had pneumonia – and I would certainly have died without their care.

'Of course, it was a bit of a shock to find myself with a group of talking frogs, but I soon grew to love them very much. There are legends of strange creatures in these swamps, but no one believes them any more. I don't know what I'll tell people when I get home.

'Jonquil and Treasure were my particular nurses. But they weren't at all comfortable about what they were doing. Often they seemed nervous and agitated, and other frogs kept coming and asking, wasn't I well *yet*? I didn't know until afterwards that they wanted me to leave so they could start practising again. Jonquil and Treasure wouldn't hear of it, though, until I was completely recovered.

'Then the atmosphere became even worse. Gobi had given them the mandolin, and said it was for me! There was an awful uproar, just like now. They were torn between respect for Gobi and fear of humans; some of them regretted their kindness to me, while others, like Jonquil and Treasure and Duke, loved me as I loved them, and didn't want me to go.

'What solved the problem in the end was the fact that frogs simply can't live without singing. In their confusion and unhappiness, they sang to console themselves; this led to other songs, and I realized that these were the lovely voices I had heard in the swamp. I told Jonquil how I had heard them from so far away, and begged her to let me go and listen properly. That made up Jonquil's mind. 'If our singing led you here,' she said, 'then here is where you belong.'

'She brought me the mandolin. I tried playing it; it wasn't totally impossible, since I had already played a musical instrument. I sang, and learned to accompany myself a little. I think that was what convinced the frogs – luckily for me, I have a good singing voice. And that was that. Things just got better and better.

'My only big worry has been how I would get home again. I knew I couldn't stay here alone. I miss being with other people, and in any case how could I survive the winter? I can't hibernate! I tried to tell the frogs, but they didn't want to think past the next song, and seemed to believe that I was theirs forever. I hoped that some other human – one who knew the way back – would turn up before it got so late in the season that I had to try to return on my own.

'Well, he did turn up – map and all – and the frogs were terrified he would take me away. Which he will do – but it looks as if we'll return together in the spring! Isn't it wonderful? That's my story!'

'What an adventure!' exclaimed Phyllis. 'Then he didn't really steal the mandolin at all?'

'Of course not. I lent it to him, in a way. I was practising right here in the clearing – and wishing, as usual, that I had someone to teach me to play really well – and suddenly, there was Joheres! It was a strange moment. I've never been so – transfixed. We stared at each other for a minute, and then he said, "Please, could I try playing your mandolin?' He seemed to know how to play it without even thinking. As it turns out, though, he's a musician, so that's not surprising. He said, "I heard you singing with the frogs last night. It was the most wonderful music I've ever heard. Could I join you?" '

'I was thrilled, but explained to him that the frogs would be terribly angry that he was even here. Joheres said, "Maybe if I practise, and become really good with the mandolin, they'll accept me." '

'That was as far as we got. I went into the bower to get some leaves, to show him how to polish the mandolin. For some reason it sounds even better when it's polished. Then one of the handmaidenfrogs came past and saw him, and that was that. I suppose you've heard *their* version of the story. I couldn't bear to tell the frogs what had actually happened, until I had had a chance to talk to Joheres again. They were already too upset, and I hadn't even asked Joheres if I could go home with him. For all I knew, he was as lost as I.'

'Gobi told me the new mandolin is for Joheres,' said Hilary. 'They won't have any choice but to accept him.'

'It's really for me then?' said Joe, appearing with Yop in the doorway of the hut. 'What an honour! Is it ready yet? Did you talk to Gobi today?'

'He told me we could pick it up on the way to the camp,' said Hilary.

'I still don't understand everything Yop has been telling me about you, Joe,' complained Phyllis. 'I'm

137

going to miss you, if you're not coming back with us. Oh, no! What are we going to tell Mother?'

'I'll just mysteriously disappear,' said Joe. 'Let's leave this smelly place and go and have supper. Yop is going to tell you all about me.'

19
The End of the Day

The mandolin was waiting for them on the shore, with Yop's chunk of goldwood. It gleamed faintly in the afternoon sun. Joe picked it up and stroked its strings gently, his eyes shining and a little damp, as everyone commented on its beauty. Hilary looked around, but as she had fully expected, Gobi was not there. She bit her lip, picked up her burdens again, and led the way back to camp.

'What are you going to tell the frogs?' asked Phyllis. She stirred up the ashes and started to build a new fire.

'I'll tell them the whole story tonight,' said Chrys. 'I've already asked Jonquil to explain that Joe Harris the gardener and Joheres the supposed thief are one and the same, so they'll be partly prepared.

'I've also suggested to Man and Kas that they gather what frogs they can – those who realize how much we owe to you all, I said – to sing a song for you before you go. You proved beyond a doubt how good humans can be, but many of the frogs are still unwilling or unable to accept that. After you've gone, I'll explain to them about Joheres and me, and that we'll have to leave as well before long. But we'll come back in the spring.' She paused, shrugging. 'I hope they'll believe that!'

When the meal was ready and they all sat down to eat, Joe said, 'Well, Yop? What do you have to say?'

'I don't know *everything*,' said Yop modestly. 'In fact, I want to ask you something first. Is this really another world from ours, or are we just someplace else on Earth?'

'It's definitely another world,' answered Joe. 'I spent some time in your public library. Your history and geography are not at all the same as ours. But what's interesting is that although the details are different, there are plenty of similarities between the two worlds – kings, countries, war, peace, discoveries, religions . . .'

'Sort of parallel worlds!' said Yop. 'Maybe that's why we feel so at home here. But what made you come to the Great Pond in the first place?'

'Just a different kind of holiday,' said Joe.

'Why not? OK, we've already been told how you met Chrys, and that you didn't really steal the mandolin. I worked out this afternoon that it must be a human being who played the mandolin, but that was all I knew about that. It never occurred to me that they were keeping Chrys a secret because they were afraid other humans would take her away.

'When you were setting off all the fireworks, it was to keep the frogs away until you had had a chance to practise.'

'Quite right,' said Joe. 'It didn't work.'

'And you were using fuses so you could be in one place while a firecracker went off somewhere else. To confuse the frogs about where you were.'

'How did you work that one out?'

'By a line of ashes on the rock,' said Yop.

'Observant, aren't you?' said Joe. 'I had wiped out all traces of the fuse that set off the firework when we arrived here, but you didn't give me a chance to get rid of the new ashes.'

'Wait!' said Phyllis, chewing and swallowing quickly and wiping her face. 'Who set off the firework that went off just after we got here? You didn't have a chance to set it up, or light a fuse then!'

'I had done that two weeks before,' said Joe.

'What! –'

'Remember what Man told us?' said Yop eagerly. 'That we would arrive home only a second after we left? It works the other way, too. Man and Joe also arrived back in the Great Pond a second after *they* left. Do you see?'

'No-o,' hesitated Phyllis.

'It was like this. Joe put the firework high up on the cliffs. By the way, why did you have fireworks, Joe?'

'To use as flares in case I got lost. I have some proper flares, too, but I wouldn't have used them. They're only for emergencies. Luckily, the firecrackers were in the knapsack I was wearing when I met Chrys. The flares are in the boat.'

'All right,' continued Yop. 'Joe set up the firework, ran the fuse down along the edge of the island, lit it, and then came through the whirlpool to our own little pond.'

'You must have had an awfully long fuse,' said Hilary. 'We were in the Great Pond for quite a while before it went off. And why did you light it, if you were planning to go to our world?'

'That was an accident,' said Joe. 'I didn't know about

your world. It *was* a very long fuse, zigzagged for much of the way up the island. After using it I had only one small piece left for yesterday morning.'

'That's why there weren't any fuses in the tree!' exclaimed Yop. 'And it also explains why the ashes spread so wide farther down – there were more of them.'

Joe laughed. 'I needed such a long fuse because I wanted to get close to the Maiden's Island before the firecracker went off. If the frogs thought I was at the whirlpool end of the island, I might have been able to get to the Maiden's Island to see Chrys without being noticed. But I ended up in your world instead. Can you guess how it happened?'

'Oh, I know!' said Phyllis and Hilary at once. Yop smiled with satisfaction.

'Right. Just like you, Phyllis, I slipped on the mud! But unlike you, I had a mandolin in my hand, which made it difficult for me to grab anything. Also, I had no reason to feel that I was in danger, and was sucked through the whirlpool before I knew what was happening.'

'You got plenty of time to practise the mandolin in our world,' said Phyllis. 'But how did you know what to do, or where to go?'

'All I really had to do,' said Joe, 'was get enough food to survive, and stay near the little pond so I could go back whenever I was ready. Of course, I didn't know for sure whether I *could* return, but I wasn't in a hurry to try. Why rush into the same mess I had just got out of?

'I came out of the woods into your back garden. You were all there at the pool, so I watched and listened, to find out what kind of place I was in. I've done a lot of gardening, and I could see there was plenty of work to be done.

'You know what happened next. It threw me a little off balance when everyone called me Mr Harris. When I said my name wasn't Mr Harris, you assumed you should call me Joe! Joheres is all one word.' He wrote it for them in the sand.

'I'll still think of you as Joe,' said Phyllis.

'That's fine. I camped down by the little pond,' continued Joe. 'I really *am* used to sleeping in the open. One night when it rained, I slept in your shed. I had vegetables from your garden and snacks from your mother to eat. She took good care of me! After she paid me, I could buy more food if I needed it.

'Also, I got some new clothes and a haircut. My plan was to come back looking quite different, and go trampling around in a loud, vulgar way, to scare the frogs into hiding. It seemed to be the only way to keep them out of the way without hurting them.'

'And then Man came into our world, too!' said Yop. 'Did you realize that Man was a frog from the Great Pond, when you first saw him?'

'No, but I was in a frame of mind to look closely at any frog that came along. When I saw that he was growing, I was certain. I would have brought your attention to him myself, if Hilary hadn't noticed. When you were talking to him, I was hiding in the woods.

'That squashed my old plan, of course, but provided me with a much better one. You three were my passport back to the Great Pond; I would appear at the little pond just as you were leaving, insist on coming along, and no one would have any reason to suspect that I was the thief!

143

'I went to a restaurant for supper, and then returned with an excuse to do more gardening. I didn't think you would get back to the frog so quickly, judging by the way you were arguing on the way up to the house. I misjudged Hilary. She sounded so reluctant that I thought she would delay you.'

Hilary blushed. 'What I don't understand is how Man could have come through to our world *after* you did, when we all arrived in the Great Pond at the same time. What happened to the one-second rule?'

'I think,' said Yop, 'that Man must have been close to the whirlpool, but not within sight of it, when Joe went through. If Joe didn't yell –'

'I didn't,' said Joe.

'– Man might not have noticed him. If he went through a few seconds after Joe, then we could all come back at approximately the same time. Joe would have surfaced first, by the same few seconds. That's what gave him time to hide the mandolin in the mud.'

'Then that's why it took so long to go through the whirlpool,' said Hilary. 'Joe had to be back first! Gosh! I wonder what would have happened if Joe hadn't got down to our pond in time! Would we have drowned in there, waiting? I was right to be scared.' She shuddered, turned quickly away and started gathering up fishbones for the last time.

'It should be much quicker going back home,' said Joe.

'Now I see why you tried to reassure me about my mother!' said Hilary. 'You already knew how it worked.'

'Hurry and finish eating,' said Chrys. 'It's almost sunset. The frogs will be ready soon.'

They all looked up at the sky. For the third day in

144

a row, the sunset was a blaze of fire. A few pink a
grey clouds stretched themselves flamboyantly across
the glowing sky, over the dark line of the swamp. The
world of the Great Pond seemed to wrap them in its
gentle heat. This is home too, thought Phyllis, but we
have to leave it.

'Only a few more questions,' said Yop. 'Why did
you set off another firework the morning after we got
here?'

'Oh dear,' said Joe, looking embarrassed. 'I wish you
hadn't asked me that!' He paused, and then continued
ruefully, 'I was just trying to keep you kids busy. I
thought it would wake you up and get you excited
about searching for the thief, and I would be able to
get on with my own plans.

'I wanted to get the mandolin out of the mud without
being seen. I spent the whole morning making my
disguise, and intended to set off another firework in
the afternoon, right by the whirlpool. If only I could
get the frogs out of the way for a few seconds, I could
pick up the mandolin and get back from the shore
before having to act like a bush once more.

'Just when I was close enough to set off a firecracker,
Phyllis appeared. She got into conversation with the
frogs. I suppose I became a little careless. I thought
they were so caught up with talking to her that they
wouldn't notice me.

'It was a terrifying moment when Phyllis slipped on
the mud. As soon as I saw that she was going to be
safe, I went into the woods. How did you know, Phyllis,
that I doubled back to the shore?'

'One of the frogs saw you,' said Phyllis.

'What made you go for the mandolin first thing this
morning?' asked Yop. 'Did we make you suspicious?'

'Not by anything specific that you did. But I know how observant you are. You had asked me earlier whether there was anything else hidden in the tree, and I wondered if you had guessed about the fuses. Then you went off and talked to Phyllis for so long last night . . . There was no reason why you shouldn't have, but I just wanted to check.'

Joe stood up and said seriously, 'I'm sorry I didn't confide in you all from the start. I felt I couldn't give all the frogs' secrets away without at least consulting Chrys. The frogs were upset enough as it was, and I didn't want to make things worse.'

Supper was over. They tidied the camp and gathered their few belongings. Yop stuffed the piece of goldwood into the knapsack with the little stones, other items went into the tent bag, and once again Phyllis strapped the sandals to her belt. Then they all waded over to the stage to hear the farewell song.

A multitude of frogs was gathered on the stage. Man and Kas, Uka and Andu stood in front, directing the choir. Man looked confused between happiness and sorrow, and Kas was peaceful; Andu and Uka appeared disgruntled but determined to play their parts. On a raft beside the stage Duke lay very still while Treasure bathed him continually with water.

Little frogs, some with colourful garlands, all with pulsing spots, jumped about with excitement and tuned their throats. The Maidenfrog climbed up behind them and took her mandolin, which the frogs had polished and floated across the water, and held it up jubilantly against the sky. Chrysanthemum shone with her mandolin, the sunset glowed, and the whole froggy choir seemed enveloped in light. Even Yop held his breath for a second at the splendid sight, and then let the feeling pass away.

'It's not quite the same with one of our directors missing,' said Man. 'We can fill the gap made by the loss of Duke, but we can't be as strong without him. We hope our songs will help to heal him.'

It is impossible to adequately describe the song of the Froggy Choir. It was as sweet and clear as a minuet, as strong and boisterous as rock, as full as a symphony; it was friendly, joyful, moving and tremendous fun. Yop stood back and enjoyed it, Phyllis cried, Hilary tried to think but couldn't, and Joheres imagined how he would fit into that wonderful song.

'Goodbye!' said the frogs. 'Thank you!'

Man leaned forward and kissed Phyllis, and Phyllis kissed him back. Chrys jumped down from the stage. 'I'll come with you to the whirlpool,' she said.

'Wait.' A thread of a voice came from behind them. It was Duke. 'I'm sorry,' he said. 'I love her so much, you see.' He fell back on to his raft.

The five humans walked silently to the whirlpool, their hearts full. Then Chrys hugged everyone and stood, arms clasped with Joe, as Yop and Hilary and Phyllis joined hands.

'Goodbye! Goodbye!'

The three adventurers climbed up through the woods. They met their mother (and Auntie Jane) coming across the lawn.

'Oh, good heavens, you're so dirty! What happened?'

'We went into that pool down in the woods,' answered Phyllis.

Mother scolded and fussed, and then looked around. 'Where's Joe? I thought he went down here, too!'

'We didn't see him, either going down to the pond or coming back up,' said Yop truthfully.

'I wonder where he can have gone –' She stopped and looked carefully at Hilary. 'You look exhausted,' she said.

'I'm so tired,' said Hilary. She put her arms around her mother and squeezed her tightly. 'It's been a long, long day.'

About the Author

Barbara Larkin was born in Vancouver, Canada. She received a Bachelor of Arts degree in English Literature from the University of British Columbia, Vancouver, and later worked in a library and studied linguistics. She is a Bahá'í and now lives near Atlanta, Georgia with her husband and three daughters. She is interested in education and uses themes in the story to introduce moral concepts and spiritual questions in a manner children can understand. The Secret of the Stolen Mandolin is her first novel.